THE SOLITARY CARPENTER

Also by Michael J. McCann

THE SOLITARY CARPENTER

A TOM FAUST CRIME NOVEL

MICHAEL J. MCCANN

THE PLAID RACCOON PRESS
2025

ISBN: 978-1-927884-34-8 (paperback)
eBook ISBN: 978-1-927884-35-5 (e-book)

Cover image: Lad Fury from Pexels
Author photo: © 2019 by Michael J. McCann

Visit the author's website at www.mjmccann.com

To Reg and Kathy Coffey
with thanks for
their unflagging support

PART ONE

THE ATTEMPT

Tom Faust pulled up at the mouth of the driveway and stopped, lowering his window as the Ontario Provincial Police constable walked around the front of his car. He handed over his private investigator's licence and waited patiently as the man found his name and jotted down the particulars on his clipboard, then held it out for Tom to sign.

"Cage Intelligence Group. Pay any good?"

"Not bad." Tom handed back the pen. "Coroner still here?"

The constable shook his head. He tucked the clipboard under his arm and moved the barrier aside, allowing Tom to enter.

The driveway was typical of country farms in Ontario, a long stretch of wheel tracks separated by a shallow moss-covered hump. Trees lined each side of the lane before suddenly giving way to a broad clearing. The house, a large Victorian brick home with bay windows, gables, and a neat verandah, loomed in front of him.

On the left were the gazebo and rows of chairs that had been set up for the wedding. On the right, a few vehicles remained in the field roped off as a parking area for the guests, most of whom had been released from the scene by now and allowed to go home.

Tom pulled up beside an OPP SUV and parked.

He found the sergeant at the side of the house where an interior perimeter had been marked off with fluttering yellow crime scene tape.

Tom knew him slightly, back when he'd been a provincial constable and Tom had been a detective inspector. Now here he was, with chevrons on his shirt and the responsibilities of an incident commander deepening the furrow at the bridge of his nose.

What was his name again? Klaussen? Klausner?

"So what brings you out to this neck of the woods, Faust?"

Krauss. Jerry Krauss.

"My boss's wife, actually. Mrs. Brenda Cage. I believe she's here with our clients, the Rushes."

Krauss nodded. "She's still around here somewhere. Clients for what?"

"I just got here," Tom said, irritation slipping into his voice. "You probably know a lot more than I do right now."

"Well, that's what they pay me the big bucks for, ain't it?"

"Who's the case manager?"

"Detective Inspector Greene."

"Kate?" He looked around for her.

"Inside."

"Detectives?"

"Paisley and Leonard."

"Don't know them."

Krauss looked at him, saying nothing. Tom got the message.

"Victim?"

"Name of Irwin Dessler. Fifty-six, home address in

Markham, occupation literary agent. Killed by a crossbow bolt in the neck. He—"

"A *what?*"

"Go talk to Kate."

Tom shrugged. "Guess I'd better."

On the front verandah, Tom was stopped by a constable with a hard look in her eyes.

"I'm expected," he said.

"So's the pope."

"Tom, come on in."

It was Kate Greene, tapping the constable on the shoulder.

"Nice to see you again," he said, following her into the front hallway.

"Same here. How's retirement?"

"Busy."

Kate had been a colleague before Tom had pulled the pin, a fellow OPP detective inspector and major case manager who would now be pushing 55 with more than fifteen years in with the Criminal Investigation Branch. She was of medium height, on the skinny side, and a touch bowlegged. Tom often wondered if she had an enemy in the world. She was immensely popular within the CIB, and coroners welcomed her with open arms when she appeared at their crime scenes.

"You'll want to touch base with your boss," she said.

"Boss's wife."

"Your boss, like I said. Follow me."

The living room was furnished with antiques and collectibles, a nineteenth-century throwback that Tom found a little too cluttered and claustrophobic for his taste. A middle-aged couple sat together on the chesterfield. Tom figured they were the Rushes, parents of the bride and owners of the farm.

Their main cash crop, if he understood it correctly, was gladiolas that they sold to florists in Peterborough, Campbellford, Stirling, and other towns in the area.

Another woman, about the same age as Mrs. Rush, got to her feet and held out her hand.

"We haven't met. I'm Brenda Cage."

He shook her hand. It was a firm, assertive grip.

"Sean has said some very good things about you, so that's why I asked him to send you down."

Unlike her husband, who'd never lost his Cockney accent, she spoke with the same cultured tones Tom had heard coming from the royal family whenever they appeared on television.

She took his elbow. "Let's step outside for a moment."

They crossed the room to a pair of French doors that opened out onto a side verandah. She closed the doors behind them.

"How much did Natalie tell you?" She took a pack of cigarettes out of her clutch purse and offered it to him. He shook his head. She lit one, inhaled deeply, and put the pack away.

"Almost nothing," Tom said. "She had to take another call. Said there'd been a homicide and you were at the scene. Gave me the address and told me you'd explain. That was pretty much it."

Natalie Stone was the vice president of Investigations at Cage Intelligence, and as such, Tom's supervisor. A former OPP senior manager, she'd recruited him a couple of years ago, shortly after he'd retired. His assignments normally came from her, but apparently Mrs. Cage was calling the tune at the moment.

He frowned, watching her hand tremble slightly as she raised the cigarette to her lips. "Are you all right?"

"Yes, of course I'm all right. Why wouldn't I be all right?

They're a mess, though." Pointing with her chin in the direction of Mr. and Mrs. Rush. "Melissa and I are old friends. I was honoured to be invited. This isn't the sort of thing they imagined happening when they left Toronto for a life of peace and quiet in the country."

Tom didn't know Mrs. Cage, and he didn't have much of a read on her at this point, but he wasn't going to pussyfoot around. It wasn't his way.

"I don't understand why we're taking on the Rushes as clients," he said. "Kate Greene's an extremely capable case manager, and although I don't know these detectives, I know—or knew, I guess—the Northumberland detachment. They're competent people. I'm not sure why they'd need our help."

"Good lord, man. You've got it completely screwed up." She folded her arms. "The Rushes aren't our client. Why would they be?"

Tom didn't know how to answer that one, so he said nothing.

"Look, I haven't meant to keep you in the dark. I don't know how you investigator types do your briefings. I'm just married to the guy, if you know what I mean. As I told Sean, though, there's something wrong here, and we need to look into it."

"Okay."

"Ken was supposed to show up along with poor Dessler, but at the last moment he decided not to come." She waved her cigarette back and forth like a conductor's baton. "In light of what's happened, it was perfectly understandable. And given all the death threats that have been flying around, it's not surprising someone's lost their life."

Tom's irritation level was steadily rising. Maintaining an even tone of voice, he said, "May I ask a question, Mrs. Cage?"

"Brenda. Call me Brenda." A drag on the cigarette, and a quick prompt to the strings section. "Ask away."

"Who the hell *is* our client?"

"Kenneth Napier."

Tom looked blankly at her.

"A friend of mine." She looked at him expectantly. "The filmmaker? Academy Award winner? Any of this ring a bell?"

"Can't say it does. Sorry."

"You'll catch up. You'll have to, because as of right now, no one knows where Ken is."

Tom's frown deepened.

"And it's going to be your job to find him."

CHAPTER 2

"Never heard of this guy," Tom said as he stepped out onto the verandah with Kate Greene. "But apparently Ken Napier's my assignment."

"And our victim was his agent?"

"Looks like it." He followed her out onto the lawn.

She turned and folded her arms, looking at the house. "Yeah, he was Robert Rush's, too. Rush writes historical romances. I actually have one lying around the house somewhere."

Tom grunted.

"Not that I'm in a hurry to get him to sign it for me."

Stepping out onto the lawn, Tom looked up at the clear blue May Day sky. "Okay, Kate. I hope I've made it clear I'm not directly involved in your case. But do me a favour and answer a few questions, will you?"

"If I can."

"What the hell is the deal with the crossbow?"

She chuckled. "I'll show you." Leading the way across the front of the house, she looked at him over her shoulder. "The daughter, Mary Ellen, and her new husband, Ted Kirk, both belong to one of those Renaissance societies. You know, medieval fairs and jousting tournaments and all that stuff."

Glancing back at the gazebo, Tom realized it was decorated with the kinds of pennants and streamers and banners that one would expect to see in a movie about King Arthur and his knights. "Whatever turns your crank, I guess."

"Mary Ellen's twenty-eight and Ted's twenty-six. She's an investment counsellor and he's a software engineer, both living in Ottawa. They chose today deliberately for their wedding, and had a bunch of events planned for the back field later on."

"May Day."

"Yeah. A big May pole with the ribbons, tables for people to sit and weave flower garlands, that kind of thing. Everybody wore costumes. Very colourful."

They rounded the house and stopped just outside the tape. Kate pointed at a long table set up near the back of the house.

"An impressive display of weapons," she said, "all historically accurate, according to Ted, although they're all working reproductions. No wooden props."

"Christ."

"Swords, halberds and pikes, axes, a bunch of knives, and bows and arrows. They were going to have an archery contest."

"And a crossbow, I take it."

"Yeah."

Tom frowned. "Isn't that something you'd have to know how to use? Since we're talking about a weapon of opportunity?"

She smiled patiently. "Yeah, Tom. It probably is."

So they'd be looking for someone who was either an experienced bow hunter, someone who used a crossbow to hunt moose, for example, or else one of these medieval enthusiasts who was trained in how to operate the weapon. Tom mulled it over until he saw Kate grinning at him.

"Once a cop, always a cop," she said.

"Sorry, I'll butt out. Do you want me to talk to your detectives before I go?"

"Do you have anything to tell them?"

"Not at the moment."

"Let us know what you find out, okay? Be a good witness, now."

"Sure."

They shook hands. She patted his wrist and walked away.

"Tom! Just a minute!" It was Mrs. Cage, coming down the verandah stairs.

What the hell did she want now?

CHAPTER 3

Craig Norwood drove westbound on the 401 with the cruise control set to a staid 110 kilometers per hour in order to avoid unwanted attention from any OPP cruisers policing the highway.

By the time he reached Bowmanville, he'd gotten his emotions under control and had stopped beating himself up for having committed such a fuck-knuckle error, but his mood remained foul as the kilometers rolled past.

Once he'd made the decision to do this kind of work for a living, years ago, he'd sworn to obey a hard-and-fast rule: no more personally motivated violence. That kind of stuff had to be left behind, in the past. No more emotional outbursts, no more vendettas, no more grudges. Strictly professional. By the book. Get the contract, do the deed, get paid, move on.

It was a rule that had served him well throughout his career. He'd made a lot of money as a cool-headed, reliable operator. A *hell* of a lot of money. And this wasn't the time to throw it all away on a fool's errand. Trouble was, he didn't see where he had much of a choice.

He'd gone there today to hoist the guy and take him

somewhere to make him talk. He found him looking at the junk on the weapons table at the side of the house, all alone, but when he reached for his arm, the guy pulled away and ran like a fucking jackrabbit toward the cars. Norwood's hand flew up, hitting himself on the mouth.

Then, quite simply, he lost his temper. Pain seared his lips and sent him over the edge. For the first time in a long time. He grabbed the nearest thing, a crossbow, cocked it, inserted a bolt, and let it fly, nailing the fucker right in the back of the neck from a distance of about ten meters.

Great. Now the guy wouldn't be telling him anything.

He passed the second exit to Bowmanville and convinced himself to shut up and focus on doing a reset. A hard reboot, Craig.

Next steps.

With Dessler no longer available to tell him what he needed to know, he had to come up with another source. The best way to do that?

A short stretch of highway passed beneath his van before he decided that he would backtrack along the route he'd followed to find Dessler in the first place. Take a fresh look at the people he'd talked to, the things they'd said, the crap he'd plowed through online looking for something that would help him.

In his haste to catch Dessler, he may have overlooked something.

He followed the 401 into Etobicoke, slowing when the traffic slowed, accelerating when it loosened up for a moment, until he finally reached the Dixon Road off-ramp, where he exited. A block and a half later, he turned into the entrance of his apartment building and let himself into the underground parking level.

He rented two spaces, one for the van and the other for his Lexus, which he parked next to. He'd already gone over the van, peeling off the magnetic signs on the side that advertised an Ottawa gardening service. His pretext for gaining access to the wedding had been that his company was subcontracted for all the landscaping, and he was personally ensuring that everything had been taken care of to his strict specifications.

He'd put the signage, his clothing, boots, gloves, and everything else in a garbage bag, which he weighted with stones and dropped into a river under a bridge somewhere between Campbellford and Mayersburg. The usual protocol.

He locked the van and rode the elevator up to the sixteenth floor.

The building was a twenty-two floor high-rise in the Kingsview Village neighbourhood of Etobicoke. It was only ten minutes from Pearson International Airport, which Norwood found very convenient for assignments that took him away from home, particularly when he travelled for a job outside the country. As far as demographics were concerned, this neighbourhood was a mixed bag of Somalis, Asians, Italians, and others. He found it very easy to blend in and disappear.

As he unlocked his condo door, he felt a familiar calmness pass through him.

Back in control. Follow the process.

Find Kenny Napier. Do the deed. Destroy anything he might have lying around. Bug out. Move on to a new contract.

CHAPTER 4

Tom looked around the place as he waited for Brenda Cage to catch up to him. It was a nice property, twenty acres or so, just the right size for a small hobby farm that would accommodate a few acres of gladiolas, a few more in pumpkins and squash, and the rest in hay to be sold to a neighbouring farmer.

Back when Tom first started working the area as part of his Central Region beat, it was known as Seymour Township. Campbellford, ten minutes away from where he stood right now, was its primary community. A year or so later, it was amalgamated into the municipality of Trent Hills along with Percy Township, which featured Warkworth and its medium-security federal penitentiary as a main attraction, and the village of Hastings, a picturesque little settlement sixteen kilometers west of Campbellford on the Trent River.

It was nice country, with plenty of rolling hills and snaking ridges left behind by the glaciers that had passed through on their way to oblivion ten thousand years ago. The municipality as a whole was home to about twelve thousand people, about 94 percent of whom were English-speaking Caucasians on the lower end of the economic scale.

Tom had worked several cases here in his time, but only one homicide. Actually, a murder-suicide involving an elderly couple, both of whom were terminally ill. Otherwise, there had been several sexual assaults and missing persons cases that had occasionally brought him down from Orillia to the Campbellford satellite office of the Northumberland detachment.

He liked being here. It was the way he'd always imagined the English countryside to be, with mostly quiet people and mostly pleasant scenery to take one's mind off the horrible things human beings were capable of doing to one another.

"A few more things to cover," Brenda Cage said, slightly out of breath after her hurried trek across the lawn.

"Yes, ma'am."

"Bloody hell. Look, I wanted to say to you that when I referred to Ken as our client, that wasn't technically accurate. My apologies. I'm not really well versed in your parlance. He's what you fellows would call a protectee, I think it is. Our actual client, the kind gentlemen paying the bill for our services, is James Alan Gould."

Tom shrugged.

"I keep forgetting you're a cop. Gould's the president and CEO of the Sloan and Gould publishing company, the ones who are putting out Ken's book. Jimmy and I are friends, you see, and hubby's taken it on as a personal favour to me."

"The investigation of Irwin Dessler's murder?"

"Lord, no. The protection of Kenneth Napier." She sighed. "You should start looking for him by contacting his manager. He likely knows where Ken is. I couldn't imagine them not staying in touch."

Tom was a little confused. "Isn't his manager dead? Didn't

they just take his body off to the morgue?"

Brenda mirrored his confusion. "What? What the devil are you on about?"

"Dessler's dead, Mrs. Cage. I'm not sure what you want me to do."

She threw back her head and barked a short laugh. "Dessler! Dessler wasn't his manager. He was his literary agent, the poor sod. *Kendrick's* his manager."

"Kendrick."

She rapped him on the shoulder with the side of her fist. "It's a good job you're good looking, Tom. Ken's *manager* is Judd Kendrick. Has his office in Markham. A real hotshot, apparently. I don't know the man, myself, but Ken has spoken highly of him. There's an entertainment lawyer on the team, too, but I don't know their name. Ken does his own contracts, so the lawyer's not really part of the inner circle, but Sean's people might be able to put you in touch."

"I'll manage," Tom said, a little stiffly.

She smiled back. "I'm sure you will."

CHAPTER 5

The following morning, Tom turned off Highway 7 at Town Centre Boulevard in Markham and worked his way north to Apple Creek Boulevard, where he swung a left and drove down a few blocks to the business park where Judd Kendrick's office was located.

He parked in the visitors' lot in front of Kendrick's building and went inside. After calling upstairs, the woman behind the reception desk told him apologetically that Mr. Kendrick would be down in about ten minutes. Tom assured her that that would be fine.

There were comfortable-looking chairs to sit on while he waited, but Tom preferred to stand, staring out the window into the parking lot.

The car he was driving was a rental, a nearly-new Toyota Camry he'd picked up in Peterborough this morning. His expense account would cover it, and he preferred to leave his beloved Town Car at home when he travelled any distance while on business.

As cars went, it was okay. Serviceable. But it was a Toyota, and as such a long way from any retired law enforcement officer's first choice in a ride.

The drive so far had clocked just over 110 kilometers to get here, and he'd arranged to keep the car for several more days, fully expecting to track down Kenneth Napier and find out what the hell was going on. So there was no use adding wear and tear to his personally owned vehicle—his baby—if it wasn't necessary.

"Tom Faust, I'm Judd Kendrick."

Tom turned around. Striding toward him was a tall, slender, thirty-something fashion model sporting a black suit, white shirt, black tie, and brown shoes. He'd evidently lost his razor three or four days ago and had given up the search. His hair was dark and carefully mussed, and the hand he held out to Tom was long and thin. His watch wasn't a Rolex, Tom noted. A Patek Phillipe, if he wasn't mistaken. Tom had seen his share of counterfeits over the course of his career, but this one looked like the real deal. Very attractive, and very, very expensive.

Tom flashed his licence, but Kendrick barely glanced at it. He took his business card and gave it the same treatment.

"Thanks for taking the time to see me," Tom said. It was something he was still getting used to saying. As a police detective, his experience had always been that people saw him when he wanted to see them or else had a damned good reason why not. Now, he had to pretend to be beholden to them for taking a few minutes out of their precious day to talk to him.

As they rode up the elevator, Tom listened to Kendrick chatter away about the importance of indie filmmaking to our cultural identity, the current economy and how difficult it was these days to squeeze a few bucks out of investors, and how important it was to manage people's expectations while blowing a little smoke up their ass at the same time.

As he followed Kendrick out of the elevator into the vestibule of his suite of offices, Tom thought about the classic line uttered by Denis Leary in *The Ref,* which he watched faithfully every Christmas with Kelly: "What are we, girlfriends? Do I give a shit about this? No."

They settled into comfortable chairs in his office and Kendrick's assistant or secretary or whatever he was came in unbidden with strong black coffee in china mugs. Tom nodded his thanks, crossed his legs, and sipped. Damned good.

"I know how cops love their coffee," Kendrick grinned, watching his reaction. "I buy it right here in Toronto from a local roaster. Hand-crafted, Sumatran artisan, obscenely cheap. I'm addicted, I swear."

"It's good," Tom admitted.

"Sure is. Now, how can I help you?"

"I'm looking for Kenneth Napier. Do you know where he is right now?"

Kendrick nodded. "When you called to make the appointment, you didn't say what you wanted to see me about. So after I green-lighted Bobby to go ahead and set it up, I made a few calls. It's what I do, right? Network. You work for Sean Cage. The Cage Intelligence Group."

"That's right."

"I have a contact there, in management. Well, I was going to say her name but I won't. I don't want to get her in trouble. Anyway, I'd already heard about what happened to Irwin, and I thought she might be able to tell me why someone from her company wanted to see me right after it happened, so she told me you'd been assigned to look after Ken. I was going to say babysit, but that's too condescending. Considering the threats that have been going around lately."

"You understand I can't babysit him if I don't know where he is, right?"

Kendrick patted the air with an elegant hand. "I get it, believe me. I totally get it. But I'm just a little reluctant to reveal his location right now."

"Tell me about this book he's writing."

"It's his autobiography. I was the one who set him up with Irwin in the first place. I don't do book deals."

Tom drank a little more coffee. It was still damned good. "If you don't mind me asking, what *do* you do?"

Kendrick set down his coffee mug and settled back in his chair. "It's a really fascinating job, believe me. Like I said, I'm a networker, right? Every day I'm reaching out, developing new contacts, massaging old ones, playing the game. Only in my case, I work the film industry. On behalf of my clients. I have five in the stable right now, but only one of them's won an Oscar. Our man Ken."

"So I've been told."

Kendrick studied him for a moment, as though gauging the degree of seriousness with which Tom was treating him. "It's a huge deal, that gold statue. Makes the money so much easier to coax out of wallets."

"So that's what you do? Get people to invest in his projects?"

"No, sorry, I've managed to mislead you without intending to. Ken does all his own fundraising, which is why he doesn't bother with an agent. Contracts, bankrolling, he handles all that. I'm farther upstream. I beat the bushes for potential investors, pardon the mixed metaphors. I also help Ken in the early stages of a project, giving advice and guidance on which film he should do next and which one could wait for a better window. Maybe suggesting a crew member who might be best for the one he decides to run with."

"Career advice?"

"He looks to me for that, yes. He trusts my instincts and my take on the industry."

Tom drained his coffee mug and put it down. "So what about this entertainment lawyer? Where does he fit in?"

"She, actually. Vanessa Black. My wife."

Tom raised an eyebrow.

"If you want to talk to her, I'll give her a call. She's in the building, one floor down."

"Convenient."

Kendrick smiled, picking up his cellphone. "Van? No, I know. I don't need it until this afternoon. Look, do you have a few minutes to talk to someone? No, about Ken Napier. Right. Yeah. Fifteen? I'll send him down when we're done. Thanks, Van."

He put down the phone. "More coffee?"

Tom shook his head. "So, am I correct in assuming you're in constant contact with Napier?"

"Pretty much. Once a day."

"He knows what happened to Dessler?"

Kendrick nodded, looking upset.

"Tell me about the threats."

"They happened right after a Toronto TV station did a piece on Ken's book. It was a puff thing, designed to stoke the pre-orders. He sat for an interview, talked about having wanted to write a book for years now about how he got into the business in the first place, blah blah. The next day I got a call from somebody using one of those voice distorter things."

"What exactly did they say?"

"That I needed to convince Ken not to go ahead with the book. If I didn't he'd make me pay. And if the book was published, he'd make Ken pay."

"I don't suppose you could tell if it was a male or female."

He shook his head. "Damned scary, though. Unfortunately, I made a mistake."

"Oh?"

"I said I wasn't involved in the book. That his literary agent was looking after it."

"Did you give him Dessler's name?"

"No, but the information's out there. Anybody who can do a Google search would find out."

"So you think you made a mistake because the guy followed up on Dessler and killed him. Is that what you're saying?"

"I don't know how you could see it any other way."

"So you were threatened and Dessler was threatened. Anyone else? What about Napier himself?"

"He says not. It may be because he's gone right off the grid while he works on his book. The only other one I know of is a woman named Brooke MacPhee, and I know about her because Irwin told me about it. She's the executive editor of non-fiction at Sloan and Gould, the publisher. This time the guy said to her if they didn't drop the book he'd fire-bomb their office. MacPhee promptly called the police and they went through the whole bomb protocol thing. It was in the news. Boosted pre-orders like you wouldn't believe."

"And that's it?"

"As far as I know."

Tom gave him his best cop stare. "Where is he, Mister Kendrick?"

"He's safe. Under the radar."

"Like I already said, I can't protect him if I'm not there with him."

"I made arrangements already for someone to be there and keep an eye on him." Kendrick looked uncomfortable as he said it.

"Where'd you find this guy? The Yellow Pages?"

"Uh, no. He's a local dude, hunting and fishing guide, watchman, that sort of thing. Cliff Bruckner. I reached him through the person who owns the place where he's staying."

"Which is where?"

Kendrick stared out the window for a very long moment, then looked at Tom's business card lying on the table between them.

"A place called Oxtongue Lake. A resort up in the Muskokas."

Tom smiled. "Now that wasn't so hard, was it?"

CHAPTER 6

Tom shook hands with Vanessa Black and sat down in the visitor's chair across from her desk. He declined an offer of coffee, having already been adequately caffeinated upstairs.

In some ways, she was a perfect match for Judd Kendrick, and in others she was his polar opposite. Tall and slender, her short black hair was cut in a stylish bob, and her wardrobe had obviously been purchased in a boutique downtown whose rent would scare the absolute bejeebers out of you. Probably next door to the haberdashery where Kendrick had bought his suit.

On the other hand, her office space was about half of what her husband occupied. Tom had passed through a small outer office with filing cabinets, a computer and printer, a desk, and a secretary. All obvious hand-me-downs except for the secretary, who was clearly putting in time while waiting for her screen test.

The inner office, Vanessa's sanctum sanctorum, was likewise on the smallish size, but not cramped. The furniture was nice—better than what her secretary was stuck with, but still not something you'd call ostentatious.

She'd decorated the walls with framed posters of movie stars and celebrities from the 1930s and 1940s, and Tom was surprised to recognize two of them—a *Screen Play* cover featuring Myrna Loy and a *Movie Mirror* with Claudette Colbert—as being the same prints that his daughter Pamela had hung on her wall when she was a girl.

It made sense, he figured, since Vanessa was an entertainment lawyer and her clientele would be card-carrying members of the industry that had canonized these women.

"You want to talk to me about Kenneth Napier?" she asked, settling down and adjusting her calf-length skirt. "I haven't really done all that much for him lately, as Judd may have explained."

"What sort of things might you have done? I'm trying to understand how Napier's business works."

"I see. Well, I came on board several years ago when Kenneth decided to incorporate. This was when he'd heard about the nomination for the Academy Award, and he wanted a better financial foundation under his feet. I helped him with that. We created Tree and Leaf Productions, with Kenneth as the sole shareholder, director, and corporate officer. That's the way he wanted it."

"A one-man show."

"Yeah. After that, I stayed on as his lawyer to look after script options, cast and crew employment agreements, clearances, releases—" she was ticking them off on her fingers and had to switch hands—"licences, and financing agreements. This last one is just to get signatures on paper, of course, since Kenneth negotiates almost all of his own financing."

"Sounds like a lot to me," Tom said.

She shrugged. "He's a very smart man. He's converted most of it to boilerplate and just gets me to double-check the wording.

A lot fewer billable hours now for me, I'll tell you."

"He seems to be able to convince people to invest in his work."

"He's a good talker. Not a bullshitter—don't get me wrong. When he starts a project he has a very clear vision of what he wants it to look like when it's done, and he's very good at making other people see it, too."

"Does he sometimes say the wrong thing? Rub people the wrong way? Has he made a few enemies along the way?"

She thought about it for a moment. "I suppose he has. He's the kind of guy who does what he wants to do and says what he wants to say, and anyone who gets in his way is liable to get knocked over if they don't look out. Not physically; I don't mean that. I mean, in terms of the business. He's very bull-headed at times."

"Oh?"

"After he won the Oscar, people threw money at him thinking they were going to make millions off him, but they forgot it wasn't Hollywood and the feature film business, where tens of millions flow in during the first week alone, but independent filmmaking where, despite your track record, the market has its limitations."

"How *does* he make money, Ms. Black?"

She smiled. "You'd think a sixty-minute documentary about used-car salesmen as lower-class income earners would rake in the millions, wouldn't you? No matter how good it is, and Kenneth's *Drinking, Driving and Selling* was an outstanding film, believe me, the revenue still comes from the same places. Theatrical releases, which are damned few any more; domestic distribution; foreign distribution; DVD sales; streaming; product placement, which Kenneth generally avoids unless he's desperate. It really doesn't add up to what people think it will. Sometimes they're pretty vocal with their disappointment."

Tom pulled out his notebook and perched his glasses on the bridge of his nose. "Any names I should know about?"

She found a business card portfolio in her desk drawer and gave him a few examples. Tom didn't think any of them would make a hot prospect for investigation, but he jotted down their particulars anyway.

"I'm getting the impression," he said, putting his notebook back in his pocket, "that none of this would be likely to bother him very much."

"Not really."

"So he's not likely to be thrown off the track with this book project of his."

"Full steam ahead, that's our Kenneth." Her smile told him that despite his gnarly disposition, Napier was highly thought of in the Kendrick-Black household.

CHAPTER 7

Norwood jogged every morning to get his blood humming and his lungs pumping. When he came back into the building, he signed into the condo gym on the ground floor where he spent half an hour on light weight training to maintain his muscle tone and the range of motion of his joints.

Back upstairs, he showered and dressed, ate a light breakfast of toast, an egg, and buttermilk, and then went into his workshop.

Norwood was by trade a carpenter. He'd become interested in it as a boy when a neighbour let him help build a deck. Norwood was eleven at the time, in Grade Six, and always in and out of trouble. His father, an electrician, had given up after Norwood set fire to a stretch of tall grass and weeds at the back of the school yard. This was a month after he stole the principal's car and drove it into a ditch. Three months after he'd beaten up two kids who'd made fun of his short haircut.

The neighbour, Mr. Collins, was kind, patient, and didn't say a lot. His instructions to Norwood were quiet and to the point. *Measure like this. Measure again, and cut. Hold the hammer like this.*

To his surprise, Norwood realized while walking home after the deck was done and Mr. Collins had given him twenty bucks for his help, that he felt good. Really good. It wasn't the money, of course. Norwood could steal five times that amount in a slow afternoon at the Renfrew mall.

It was the fact that all his residual anger, the anger he carried around in his head every day and every night, had been lulled to sleep. His jaw muscles weren't tight and his hands, after working with tools all day, weren't clenched into fists, as they usually were.

He thought about the smell of the wood when he cut it. Cedar, Mr. Collins had explained. It left the sweet smell of the forest in the spot in his brain where such things are remembered afterward. It was pleasant.

There he was, age eleven, walking home to his family's rented house on Haig Avenue, making up his mind that some day he would be a carpenter.

It didn't happen for quite a while.

He made several bad friends and began doing bad things for them. He dropped out of school after finishing Grade Ten, moving into a small space at the back of a downtown garage run by a local biker gang affiliated with the Angels. He was big for his age, six feet and nearly two hundred pounds, all bone and muscle, and he could hold his own in the rough stuff.

The guy who ran the garage offered to sponsor him as a prospect. Norwood passed all their brainless tests with ease and breezed through the initiation. He was lined up with a bike and given a job, running junk to the local dealers and bringing back the cash, but he was hopeless with motorcycles. Eventually, he crashed, broke his leg and collar bone, and spent a week in the hospital. Luckily he hadn't been on a run, just a quick trip to the beer store. Otherwise he would have gone from the hospital to jail.

He was eighteen.

While rehabbing the leg, he used his bad friends to find him an apprenticeship spot with a carpenter who had ties to the gang. He worked his way up from menial tasks like site prep and toting boards around to actual carpentry work, learning the tricks of the trade until his limp was gone and his twenty-first birthday was in the rear-view mirror. He got his papers as a journeyman carpenter and starting taking freelance jobs.

He kept his gang ties active and ran the occasional errand for them. Eventually he was asked to kill someone—

That was a memory for another day.

Norwood had set up the third bedroom in his condo as a workshop. It had been a bit of a challenge, given the limited square footage he had to work with, but he'd watched a lot of YouTube videos on apartment workshops and gathered ideas on how to make it work.

Leaning on the doorframe, a fresh cup of coffee in his hand, he smelled the air of the room, which was different from the rest of the place. Sawdust; glue; stain; linseed oil.

He'd put up two cabinets on one wall, and a third on the wall to his right, above his workbench. In one cabinet he kept his finishes, paint, and glues: small cans of stain and various oils; waxes; pint-sized tins of paint in various colours; carpenter's glue; and epoxy glue. In the cabinet next to it were his hand tools, including Japanese saws, hand planes, chisels, squares, a marking gauge, levels, rulers, and a folding measuring tape.

In the cabinet above his workbench were metal working tools, wire brushes, files, and other assorted items.

On his workbench were a toolbox with drill bits, wrenches,

and pliers; a vise; a grinder; and plastic tool cabinets with assorted screws and nails, all neatly sorted, the drawers carefully labelled.

On his workbench right now was a child's rocking horse he was making for his youngest daughter, who would turn two in a couple of months. He'd found a plan on the Internet for one that had an attractive vintage look to it, complete with a leather harness and covered hooves.

He was in the middle of sanding the rockers. He'd thought about finishing them up this morning but, standing there, he changed his mind.

Right now was the time for business, not pleasure.

While backtracking on the process he'd followed to find Irwin Dessler, he kept coming back to Judd Kendrick. This guy, he decided now, closing the workshop door, would definitely be able to tell him where little Kenny was hiding out.

Or else.

CHAPTER 8

Tom drove slowly down the tree-covered lane to the resort, which was as spectacular as he'd expected. He parked at the side of the building next to an old brown-and-yellow Scottsdale truck and got out.

Oxtongue Lake, the crown jewel of the Oxtongue River Watershed, glittered on his right. According to the guy at the service station in Dorset, where Tom had bought gas and a chocolate bar, the place had been named by a Scottish surveyor named Murray, probably while craving one of his granny's ox tongue sandwiches.

Of course, the name on the guy's window was *Gallagher's Gas and Convenience*, so the origin story may have been apocryphal and intended as a disparagement toward people of Scottish descent.

All other points of the compass around the resort consisted of the same forest through which he'd driven to get here. A mix of white pine, hickory, and maple, it had first attracted logging interests before branching off into tourism in the twentieth century. It was a beautiful spot, Tom admitted. The air smelled fresh, and the light breeze was warm.

As he stood next to his car, he heard a sound behind him. He started to turn around. Something large and hard hit him on the side of his head. Down he went.

Sparks flashed in front of his eyes, but he still retained his wits. Lying on the ground, he swung his legs around and caught his assailant on the side of the knee with the heel of his shoe.

"Oww! Oww! You bastard! You broke my knee! I'll fill you full of lead!"

Getting to his knees, Tom saw that the man he'd taken down was a grizzled oldster in a plaid shirt, green Dickies trousers, and steel-toed boots. The shotgun he'd used to brain Tom lay on the ground nearby. He continued to howl, curled up in a fetal position, arms around his injured leg.

Tom picked up the shotgun and nudged him with it on the shoulder. "Come on, get up. You'll live."

"Damn it, that was my good leg you kicked!"

Tom grabbed his wrist, planted his feet, and hauled the old man upright. He held onto his arm as he staggered around, finding his balance.

"Cliff Bruckner, I presume."

"Yeah, and who the hell are you?"

"Tom Faust. What did you hit me for? Didn't they tell you I was coming?"

"Faust, is it? Sure, but how was I to know it was you? You could have been the guy coming after Ken."

"Yeah, well, I'm not. Where is he? Inside?"

"Where else would he be?"

Tom helped him through the door, where Cliff shook him off and hobbled into the great room. "This is the guy they said was coming up to see you. Knee-capping son of a bitch."

The man who shook his hand was surprisingly young

looking, despite Tom's understanding that he was in his mid-forties. He resembled the famous actor and director Ron Howard at the time he'd directed *Apollo 13*, in 1995. Except that, unlike Howard, he was still in full possession of his neatly trimmed tawny hair.

He wore a light brown jacket, a green shirt, and khaki trousers. His brown Skechers shoes were slightly scuffed. No jewelry—no watch, no rings, no bracelets. His glasses had black rims. His handshake was quick and informal. Mostly fingers.

Tom held up his licence, which Napier took and examined with interest.

"I thought they'd send somebody younger," he said, handing the licence back. "More, I don't know, physically imposing."

"What you see is what you get," Tom replied, putting the laminated licence back into his wallet.

"Sure." Napier chuckled. Dimples creased his cheeks. He glanced at Cliff, who'd fetched an elastic bandage from another room and was sitting in a leather armchair, wrapping his knee.

"Just as long as you understand, Mister Faust. This is no country for old men."

CHAPTER 9

Tom toured the resort to get a sense of the layout, the various points of entry, and whatever security it might have. Napier had resumed his work at the kitchen table, not particularly interested in anything else at the moment.

There was a typical alarm system, with a base station in the hallway, a keypad just inside the main entrance and a key fob-style remote, and alarms on the other doors, including in the kitchen, the sliding French doors from the dining room onto the deck, and sliding doors from the master bedroom onto another small deck.

Cliff had changed into Bahama shorts and a red Hawaiian shirt featuring large yellow flowers. Being an aficionado of Hawaiian shirts, Tom thought it looked pretty good, but the elastic bandage around Cliff's knee and the limp that went with it were a bit overdone.

For his part, Tom had a slight abrasion where Cliff had hammered him with the stock of his shotgun, but it hadn't bled and didn't need to be covered.

"What about external cameras, Cliff?"

Cliff eased down into a chair, wincing dramatically. "Couple of them. One over the front door and one over the sliding doors into the main bedroom. They connect to the base station. It beeps if they come on. Motion activated." He rubbed his other knee, making sure it was still functional. "I set up a trail camera on the driveway. It connects to an app on my cellphone. That's how I knew you were coming in."

"Lovely."

Tom wandered off, peeking into the kitchen to make sure Napier was undisturbed. A young woman was in there with him, emptying a dishwasher and putting stuff away. Tom went in.

"Excuse me. Who are you?"

She was young, in her early twenties. Her hair was long, mouse-brown, and very straight. She'd used a small red tie with a bow on it to pull it back into a ponytail that fell between her shoulder blades. She had freckles, and her cheeks were blushing behind them.

"I'm Elaine," she said. "You're Mister Faust, aren't you?"

"Why are you here?"

"She's Cliff's granddaughter," Napier said without looking up from his laptop.

"Mister Napier hired me to look after things," she said. "Cooking and housekeeping."

Tom leaned his hip against the kitchen counter. "Live-in or hourly?"

"She has the upstairs room at the back," Napier said. "Is that okay with you?"

Tom ignored the sarcasm, staring at Elaine. "Does everybody know you're here?"

"Everybody?" Napier repeated, finally looking up.

But Elaine was shaking her head. "I don't have a lot of friends."

"Social media?"

"I like to look at the memes and stuff, and listen to music, but I don't talk a lot on it."

"Boyfriend? Girlfriend?"

She looked embarrassed. "I'm sort of between relationships right now."

Napier snorted. "I think she probably passes the security check, Faust. Unlike some politicians we could mention. Interview over?"

Tom pushed away from the counter. "Yeah. Now it's your turn. Let's go for a walk outside."

CHAPTER 10

Tom followed Napier outside and across the recreation area, with its horseshoes and ring toss setup, badminton net, picnic table, and fire pit, to the dock stretching out into the lake. It was about five meters long, and two very inviting-looking Muskoka chairs were arranged out at the end to afford an unobstructed view of the water.

Napier took the one on the right, leaning back and crossing his legs. He ran a hand through his tawny hair, sighed, and laced his fingers together in his lap. Tom sat down in the other chair and looked at the lake.

It was worth looking at.

The small bay in which the resort sat was a horseshoe shape, with the point on the left curving out a bit toward the centre in a small peninsula. It was covered with jack pine, spruce, white pine, and a few maples squeezed in between, just beginning to produce green leaves.

Beyond the bay, Tom could see the far side of the lake. Several cottages dotted the shoreline, and the low hills behind them appeared to be a mix of birch and maple, also just coming to life in the anticipation of summer.

The water reflected the blue and white of the sky, and the green of the pines, with enthusiasm. It looked cold and clean.

"Beautiful, isn't it?" Napier murmured.

"Sure is."

Elaine came out with a tray. She handed Napier a whisky tumbler filled to the brim, and offered Tom a cup of coffee from a small pot.

"It's past three o'clock," Napier said, "so it's Manhattan time for me. I thought you'd probably pass because you're on duty. Is that still a thing, even though you're retired?"

"I don't drink."

"Admirable." Napier slurped. "God, that's good."

An early lesson Tom had had to learn as a recovering alcoholic was how to spend time in the company of people while they were drinking. Bourbon had been his preferred beverage, neat or over ice, and since it was the primary ingredient in Manhattans, he could smell it now, and the taste came back to him in a powerful tsunami. It was the same thing every time. He experienced the memory, thought about it for a moment, then pushed it aside.

"I want to talk to you about the threats," he said.

"Not right now. Let me enjoy this."

Tom bit his lip, trying to remain patient.

"I've been shooting footage in my spare time" Napier said. "I'm going to put something together about the book-writing process."

He slurped again. "I'm like a barracuda; I can't stop working. If I do, I'll drown."

"I know what you mean."

"You do?" Napier looked at him. "Yeah, I suppose you do. Career cop; pushed into retirement; old habits die hard. Look,

I'm glad you're here."

Tom nodded.

"A lot of money up here, did you know that?"

"I wasn't aware."

Napier chuckled at his terse response. "We're just outside the perimeter of the Muskokas, but the area in general has been a magnet for rich folk and their rich pals for a long time. Timothy Eaton had a summer estate up here. The model, Cindy Crawford, had a cottage on Lake Joseph. Shaquille O'Neal, the actor Austin Butler, Mark Wahlberg, Jamie Salter the Canadian billionaire"—he laughed at Tom's blank look—"Authentic Brands Group? Tie-ins with a lot of these folks. Did I mention David and Victoria Beckham? The list goes on and on."

Tom did his best not to look impressed by the who's-who of celebrity vacationers. It wasn't hard.

"But it's the artists," Napier went on, "that made this area so special, in my humble opinion. Tom Thomson, of course, haunted Algonquin Park, which is only twelve kilometers from here. His famous painting, *Northern River*, was based on sketches he made on the Oxtongue River, for example. Thomson brought several of his Group of Seven friends up here, too. He took A.Y. Jackson on a canoeing trip along the river, and Jackson's sketches of the rough shoreline were later transformed into one of his signature works, *The Red Maple*. A.J. Casson and Fred Varley were here, too."

"Interesting."

"Yeah, it is." Napier sipped, quietly this time, and stared out across the water. "It's not just some place stuck in the middle of God's asscrack, Tom. It has some history attached to it."

Tom said nothing, wanting to get back to the subject of the threats but willing to wait it out in case Napier said something relevant. It had always been a guiding principle of his that patience in an interview, whether it be a witness or a person of interest, could often bring its own reward.

"Mind you," Napier went on, "history has nothing to do with the natural beauty of this place. I could quote you all the geographical specifications of the lake, but I'll spare you the details for now."

He drained his glass and stood up.

"Tell me about the threats," Tom said. "Did you receive any yourself, personally?"

Napier looked down at him. "No. Probably because I'd gone off the grid before they started, and they couldn't find me."

Tom stood up as well in order to be at eye level with the man. "Who did get them?"

"Irwin. Judd. Brooke. That was all, I think."

"Brooke?"

"MacPhee. My editor for the book."

"What kind of book are you writing? An exposé that's going to piss off a bunch of people?"

Napier moved between the chairs and started up the dock. "Not at all. Just a basic autobiography. About a kid growing up in Renfrew who falls in love with movies and decides to make his own films. For a living. Pretty harmless stuff."

He reached the end of the dock. "Speaking of which," he said over his shoulder, "I want to get another couple of hours' work done before dinner."

Tom watched him walk through the recreation area and disappear into the building. Apparently, his other questions would have to wait.

He pulled out his phone, sat down again, and called Natalie Stone. Time to touch base with the boss.

CHAPTER 11

"**What's going on with** the Dessler investigation?" Tom asked, watching a duck paddle across the water in front of him.

"They've finished collecting all the physical evidence at the crime scene," Natalie replied. "They've interviewed all the guests and caterers and so on, and they're going back for seconds on a few of them. Area canvass turned up nothing useful. They're running down the victim's client list and talking to those people."

She paused. "They're going to want to interview Napier."

Tom watched the duck disappear underwater. "That's problematic. We need to keep him off the grid."

"I understand. But we don't want to give the appearance of obstructing their investigation."

"I know." He kept waiting for the duck to surface. It didn't.

"I'll have to talk to Roach," she said.

Tom grunted. Inspector Mark Roach was the detachment commander for Northumberland County, having transferred from Peterborough County a year ago. He and Tom had a bit of a history, having clashed during the Bushmaster investigation that pulled Tom out of retirement and into Cage Intelligence when a body was found hanging in the decommissioned church in Selwyn, north of Peterborough, that he was renovating as his new home.

Tom's opinion was that Roach was a fussy, myopic candy-ass with an inflated sense of self-importance.

"I'll get it set up," Natalie said, just as Tom spotted the duck popping to the surface close to the middle of the lake.

It arched its back, tipped its head, and began to cry at the sky. It was a sound somewhere between a crowing and a wailing.

A loon, he realized.

"Bring him in when I give you the word," she went on. "Just don't disclose his location. They don't need that. They'll want any evidence he might have relating to the threats. Does he have any?"

"No. He didn't receive any personally, so all he knows is second hand." Tom sat up suddenly at the sound of a vehicle crunching up the driveway to the resort.

"Christ, I gotta go, Nat. Visitors."

"Oh, good. That would be your protection team."

He was about to end the call, but he clapped the phone back over his ear. "What the hell are you talking about?"

The line was dead.

CHAPTER 12

By the time Tom reached the driveway, Cliff was already out there shaking hands with a man and a woman who'd emerged from their shiny black Suburban SUV. The old man hadn't brought his shotgun with him this time, Tom noted.

The male was in his late twenties or early thirties. His hair was trimmed short and his ears, which were low on his head, stuck out like jug handles. He wore a light combat jacket over a black T-shirt and camouflage trousers tucked into black combat boots. His jacket had big patch pockets, detachable sleeves that converted it into a vest, and an embroidered patch featuring the Cage Intelligence logo.

"Faust? I'm Bradley. This is Cohen."

Tom shook hands. The woman, Cohen, was in her mid-twenties but looked eighteen. Medium height; thin; long nose and pointed chin; dark eyes and eyebrows; long, dark hair tied back. She could have passed for an Israeli soldier on leave to study foreign intelligence methods.

"I'm Tom Faust," he said, offering his hand.

"Ariela Cohen." She shook his hand with a firm grip. "This isn't the protectee, I hope." She gave Cliff a disdainful glance.

"Lord, no. Napier's inside. Who do you report to?"

Bradley shrugged into a knapsack and settled it onto his back with a couple of bounces. "Bryan Weir."

Weir headed the Operational Support Division at Cage, and he also looked after the Protective Services Unit. A former captain with the Hamilton police department, he'd reached a point of near-burnout after years of dealing with organized crime in the city and had taken early retirement in exchange for a desk job working for Sean Cage.

Tom had gotten to know him since joining the organization, and they'd become friends.

"Lead the way," Bradley invited, nodding toward the cottage.

Cliff did the honours, taking them on a quick tour and gathering everyone in the great room. Bradley and Cohen dropped their knapsacks in a corner and took centre stage.

"Mister Napier," Bradley said, arms folded, "Cohen and I are your protection detail while Mister Faust oversees the process and maintains liaison with HQ. Normally you'd get four of us, but today it's just Cohen and me. This is what I call 'Protection Lite.'"

No one laughed.

"Make no mistake, though. Cohen and I are the real deal, and you'll be as safe as a baby in our hands. It's our understanding you'll be sticking here and won't need to leave the resort, so this'll be what I call static protection mode."

Tom rolled his eyes. "What I call" had always been a red flag for him, an assertion that the speaker thought he was the smartest guy in the room and wanted everyone to believe he'd invented every workable concept on the planet. Bradley was merely quoting chapter and verse from the handbook on introductory personal protection while making it sound like his own. Tom wasn't impressed.

"We'll do a site reconnaissance and come up with our risk assessment, establish a perimeter, and take it from there. We brought equipment with us. Cohen will monitor the electronic stuff and I'll patrol the exterior. Faust, you can feel free to chip in anywhere."

"Thanks."

"If for any reason you have to move," Bradley continued, "we'll transition into what I call mobile protection mode. Cohen will drive. We'll go over the protocols later."

"Good idea," Tom said.

Bradley glanced at him. "It's my hope we can stay put until this threat's resolved, but it's always important to be prepared for contingencies. Any questions?"

Napier held up his hand. "I feel like I'm being held prisoner here."

"This is Canada," Bradley replied. "At any time, you're free to walk out the door and get yourself killed. Cohen and I will probably have to find another job somewhere, but at least we'll still be breathing. Unlike you."

"Ease up," Tom murmured.

"Are you armed?" Napier asked. "I don't see your gun."

"This is a common question." Bradley glanced at Cohen and resumed his professorial tone. "The first thing you need to know is that it's not legal in Canada to hire an armed bodyguard unless it's a case of what's called 'imminent danger.' The only exceptions are for armoured car protection and people working in remote areas to protect themselves from wildlife. That's it."

"Yeah, well, somebody's trying to light up my ass, which is why you guys are here in the first place. I'd say that constitutes imminent danger, wouldn't you?"

"Yes, sir. At the moment our firearms are secured under lock and key in our vehicle. After we've set up shop and completed our reconnaissance, we'll deploy them as the situation warrants."

Napier rolled his eyes. "Well, what the hell are you going to use to protect me if this guy shows up five minutes from now? Harsh language?"

Bradley removed an expandable baton from a small scabbard on his belt. "Cohen and I are trained and proficient with these."

"We're also martial arts black belts," Cohen chipped in. "Our hands are registered as lethal weapons."

Napier snorted. "No, they're not."

She smiled. "Well, they should be."

"What about you?" Napier asked Tom. "I take it that you're not armed."

"Not unless you count the bazooka in the trunk of my car."

"Funny." Napier stood up. "I left my drink out in the kitchen. I think I need a fresh one."

"Don't worry, Mister Napier," Cohen called out to him as he left the room. "We'll take care of you."

"That's what I'm afraid of."

CHAPTER 13

Tom was stretched out on his bed, on top of the covers, listening to a CD by the 1970s Italian progressive rock band Le Orme. It was their most successful release, *Felona E Sorona*, a concept album about two planets that orbit each other while never coming in contact. Released in 1973, it was a very good example, in Tom's opinion at least, of a European combination of psychedelic rock and space rock, and he thought he could hear the influence of Peter Hammill and Van der Graaf Generator, Hammill having written an English translation of the original Italian lyrics featured on this release.

His phone, which lay on the bed beside him, began to vibrate. He picked it up, looked at the call display, and immediately killed the music.

"Pamela! How are you doing? Everything all right?"

"Everything's fine, Daddy. What are you up to these days?"

"I'm on a job, although"—he glanced at the time in the corner of the screen—"I'm getting some rest at the moment. How about you?"

"Same here, actually. I forgot about the time difference; I'm just catching up on my reading, then I'm going to order in some dinner. I'm tired."

"How's Seattle?"

"Damp. It's about 17 degrees, so that's not too bad, although the locals think they're freezing to death. Paul's got us in a really nice hotel close to the waterfront. Very comfortable and secure."

"Glad to hear it. How is he?"

"Paul?" She chuckled. "About what you'd expect. For a guy about to hit seventy, he's a bloody whirlwind."

"Is he treating you okay?"

"Yes, Daddy. He's a dream to work for."

Tom pulled another pillow behind his head and settled down into a more comfortable position. "Tell me about it."

"Well, you know he directed a couple of the Jason Bourne movies, right? Remember the triple chase scene in *The Bourne Ultimatum* and the incredible fight in the apartment? Best ever, in my book. But he's actually better known for his docudramas, like *Bloody Sunday*, *United 93*, and *Captain Phillips*."

"That's the one with Tom Hanks?"

"Yes. But now he's back doing a thriller, which is where I come in."

"Does it have a title yet? Or are they still arguing over that?"

She laughed. "The money's all lined up, so the project's settling into shape. They're calling it *Losers Weepers* after all."

When Pamela had told him a month or so ago about her next film, she'd said it was based on a novel by that name, but one of the producers wanted to call it something else. Clearly, Greengrass had won that argument. Along with many others, no doubt.

"It's in pre-production now, but Paul's a lot different than other directors I've worked for before. We're doing the script breakdown, and Paul asked me to sit in, since I'm the lead. He's very inclusive that way, and he told me he's going to expect some improvisation when we shoot."

"What's that? Script breakdown?"

She sighed. "It's like the most detailed and picky thing you ever saw in your life. We sit around a table and go through the script scene by scene, and Paul's team makes all these lists of everything that'll be needed when we move to production. Which characters will be in the shot? Which set is it? What props have to be there? Which crew members? All the answers have to be collected into breakdowns for casting, locations, scheduling, and God, a million other things."

"Sounds complicated."

"It is. I'm glad I only have to act, although a few times I've told them that something wouldn't work for my character."

"Do they listen to you?"

"You bet they do. Academy Award nominee? Excuse me."

Tom laughed, thinking of how proud he'd been watching her on television, walking up the red carpet and then sitting in the audience, waiting for the winner of the Best Actress Award to be announced. Her film, *A Turn of the Screw*, had already won an award for best costumes, and Tom remembered how excited he'd been for her. He recalled how the camera lingered on her while they were waiting for Jamie Lee Curtis to read the winner's name, and how they'd cut back to her for a reaction shot when someone else won. Her face remained carefully neutral. Her disappointment was masked the way he'd seen her hide it countless times before.

He'd never been so proud of her as he'd been in that moment.

"They've completely rewritten the script from what I told you about before. And they gave me input into that, too."

"So it's different from the book now?" Tom had actually tracked down the novel in a used book store and read it. Not his cup of tea, but he could see how it would make a good movie.

"Completely. Now I'm Maggie Adams, a single mother in Seattle. I retired from the Seattle police after a harassment complaint went wrong and got me ostracised from the force. Pretty standard stuff so far, right?"

"Okay."

"I work as a real estate agent. Then one day my daughter and I are out shopping, and she gets kidnapped while we're in a fish market. I rush around, trying to find her, and finally call the police. I'm transferred to a detective who knows me. He gives me the brush-off. Then I discover an upscale house I'm repping has been broken into and trashed. While I'm looking at the damage, I get a call. 'Give us what you stole from the house or you'll never see your daughter again.' So I take matters into my own hands, and it's all action from then on."

"You're right, that's different from the book."

She paused for a moment. "I wanted to ask you a couple of questions, Daddy."

"Sure. Anything."

"Do you know any women who were harassed on the job? Women cops?"

Tom thought for a moment. "No, not personally. I knew cases where it had happened, but I didn't know the people involved."

"What about Ellie March?"

Tom laughed. "No one in their right mind would try to harass Ellie March."

"Okay." She paused, and Tom could hear a pen scratching on paper. She was taking notes. "Can you give me some tips on how I can show an underlying vulnerability in Maggie? The script calls for her to be angry and in charge, but she still hasn't recovered from her ostracism. I don't want her to be defensive and whiny, but I want to bring out the fact that she's isolated and has nobody covering her back. I've got some ideas, but I want to hear what you say."

"Let me see." He thought for a moment. Pamela was a pro's pro and an experienced actor who already had a pretty good idea, no doubt, how she wanted to play the character. He figured she was trying to include him in her work because she loved him. Also in case he mentioned something that hadn't occurred to her before.

"It depends on what your director wants," he said, "but I'd say you could show it through your hands, for one thing."

"My hands?"

"Your character's action-oriented but trying to restrain herself at first, right? She wants the police to handle it? I've watched a lot of people in stressful situations over the years. Facial non-verbals can tell you a lot with witnesses and family members, but cops are trained and experienced enough to control their facial expressions, so I think you'd keep that to a minimum. Sometimes the stress leak outs through their hands. Trembling, say. If Maggie smokes, make your hands tremble a bit when you're lighting one."

"That's good, Daddy."

"A clenched fist. Rubbing your thumb and index finger together. Wringing your hands or squeezing your fingers. Sitting on your hands to try to control them. I've noticed things like that in people under a lot of stress."

"Okay."

"You know what you need, Pammy, is a technical advisor. An experienced female cop who can give you a personal perspective."

"Yeah! Since we're still in pre-production, we won't start shooting until October. I'm sure they'd sign the person on now and I could Zoom with them or whatever, then they could come out when we shoot and be on site."

"I might know someone. Let's park it for now and I'll get back to you."

"All right. Are you doing okay?"

"Fine. Not drinking, in case you're wondering. Seven months, two weeks, three days and, what time is it? That many hours."

"What are you working on?"

"Do you know Kenneth Napier?"

"Napier? Sure. The doc film guy."

"What's your take on him?"

"A touch of arrogance, which you need to survive in this business. No sense of humour. Money genius. Smart, smart, smart. Not much else. I've only had a few conversations with him, at parties or whatever, where everyone's playing a role anyway. Oh, and he's a bit of a drinker. Why do you ask?"

"He's writing his autobiography. The thing to do these days, I guess. Well anyways, there've been death threats over it and his literary agent was just murdered, so there's a connection. They've asked me to sit on him for a while. Central Region's looking into it."

"Death threats and a murder? I don't need to tell you to be careful, do I?"

"No, but it's always good to hear it from you."

"I'd better go now, Daddy. I love you very much."

"I love you too."

He ended the call and put the phone down, feeling better.

As his mind passed over the conversation, reviewing what he'd said to her, he suddenly thought of Napier during Bradley's protection briefing. He'd affected a nonchalance bordering on indifference, but his hands had been restless. Tom was only now calling it to mind.

Despite his casual outward demeanour, Napier was afraid.

CHAPTER 14

Norwood spent the next day, which was Saturday, surveilling Judd Kendrick's home in north Vaughan. It was a very nice house in a very nice neighbourhood, with a swimming pool and a tennis court behind a privacy fence, and a black BMW 4 coupe sitting in the driveway. A car that ran to $80K new, Norwood had read. Money, money, money.

Norwood found a spot of high ground nearby that afforded him a clear view of the Kendrick property. Forest Ridge Road was very quiet, tucked into a green area just north of Richmond Hill, and he was unworried about being noticed. He'd driven the Lexus, which blended nicely into the neighbourhood.

His pretext, should anyone stop and ask if he needed help, was that he had run out of gas and was waiting for CAA, the automobile club. It was Saturday, so it was busy, and they'd told him he might have to wait a bit. He didn't mind the delay; he had a magazine with him to read. An issue of *Road and Track*, as it happened.

He'd also shaved and dressed for the occasion, with a newish black leather jacket over a lilac-coloured mock turtleneck, Ray Ban sunglasses, and large ruby ring on his right hand. He wanted to look like money, money, money.

As it was, he spent almost ten hours in the same spot without being disturbed. Only a few vehicles passed by the entire time, mostly vans paying service calls or sports cars heading out for weekend recreation.

Kendrick was one of the latter. Norwood watched him load golf clubs into the trunk of the BMW at 9:34 AM, perhaps on his way to a ten o'clock tee-off with his buddies.

He gave it ten minutes and called the wife's number, saying he was supposed to meet Juddie at the golf course but couldn't make it, and Juddie's phone was going straight to voicemail. "Do you know where they're heading after they play?"

Vanessa Black gave him the name of the restaurant and the reservation time. Norwood thanked her and disconnected. He jotted it all down in his notebook, using his own personal shorthand and, when the reservation hour rolled around, he called the number.

It was the correct restaurant, all right, and when he asked to speak to Judd Kendrick he only had to wait a couple of minutes. Kendrick came to the phone and Norwood immediately disconnected. He tossed the book onto the passenger seat. He wasn't going to bother following Kendrick, because he didn't really care where he was, he just wanted to know how he was spending his day.

The wife, for her part, surprised him by not leaving the house for a Saturday morning outing of her own. About an hour after Judd's departure, she wandered out in a tank top and shorts and stretched out in a lounger next to the pool with a tablet in her hand. She read for twenty minutes or so before wandering back into the house, leaving the tablet on the lounger.

When she returned, she carried a tray with a large pitcher, a margarita glass, and a plate of what Norwood thought might be shrimp and cheese. She settled back down in the lounger after filling her glass, and resumed reading, pecking occasionally at the plate. Brunch, no doubt.

And so it went. She went back inside when the pitcher was empty, and this time took the tablet with her. There was nothing until a little after 3:30 pm, when Kendrick returned home. He parked the Beemer in the garage. Thirty-six minutes later he came out to the pool and swam for nearly fifteen minutes. Then he stretched out on the lounger and fell asleep.

According to the weather app on his phone, the temperature right now was 19 degrees Celsius. It was probably a little bit higher in the direct sun, where Kendrick lay snoozing. He'd read once that Torontonians generally opened up their pools for the season in the last week of April or early May. It was easier to get a service booking before the big late spring rush, apparently.

Norwood had carried out his share of poolside executions; for some reason the setting seemed to lend itself to a quick and private, in-and-out killing. But he'd thought about it all day, while sitting there reading his magazine, and he'd decided that he'd follow one of two courses. If Kendrick went out again tomorrow morning, he'd cut him off on the road, having switched to the van, and he'd take him away from there. On the other hand, if the wife went out somewhere instead, he'd gain ingress into the house and capture him there.

If they both went out together, he'd wait a day and take Kendrick on his way to work the next morning.

He ended the surveillance and, while driving back home, visualized how he'd transport Kendrick to the interrogation cabin and break the bastard's spirit before learning everything he wanted to know.

CHAPTER 15

The drive from Oxtongue Lake to Cobourg took three hours, covering a distance of 220 kilometers altogether. Cohen drove the Suburban with Bradley riding shotgun. Tom and Napier sat in the back.

Napier shot some footage out the window with his hand-held camera, tracking their progress south on Highway 35 to Minden, but when he started training the lens on Tom, and at Bradley behind the wheel, asking questions about the investigation and providing a running commentary on their serious demeanour, his fellow passengers were unanimous in their insistence that he put the camera away before it disappeared up his nether region.

Tom had made many such drives in his career, long and tedious, but somehow this one felt longer and more tedious than usual. They were heading for the Northumberland County detachment hub office where the crime unit investigating Irwin Dessler's murder was located, and Tom was more than aware that he'd likely bump into Mark Roach. He really wasn't in the mood for the man's passive-aggressive nonsense today, but there was no way around it. He was entering Roach's bailiwick, and he'd have to pay the entrance fee.

Cohen parked out front and Bradley handed Tom a push-to-talk phone. Tom went inside and asked for Detective Constables Paisley and Leonard. He hung around for five minutes or so, reading the bulletins and safety flyers posted on the wall for public consumption, until one of them—Paisley, Tom remembered—opened the inner door.

Tom called Bradley and told him to bring in Napier. He waited with Paisley and then followed the detective through the security door and down the corridor, his entourage of three close behind.

Kate Greene appeared in an open doorway and nodded. Tom nodded back. Over her shoulder he could see audio-visual equipment, indicating an observation room. They stopped in front of the next door down, which was an interview room.

"Mister Napier," Paisley said, "come with me. The rest of you, wait at the front entrance."

The door of the interview room opened. Detective Constable Leonard stood there, tapping his fingers on the doorframe.

"I'll wait right here," Bradley said.

"You'll wait up front," Leonard said.

"Move it," Tom said, nudging Bradley's shoulder.

They trudged back up the corridor, Paisley showing the way. Kate was still standing in the doorway, and when Tom reached her, she touched him lightly on the arm. He stopped.

"Is he going to be able to tell us much?"

Tom shook his head. "He didn't personally receive any of the threats, since he was already in seclusion, writing the book."

"He was aware of the others?"

"Yeah."

"Gives us a starting point."

They were standing near the men's washroom. The door

opened and Superintendent Mark Roach emerged, wiping his hands on a piece of brown paper towel.

"I heard you'd be showing up," Roach said, wadding up the paper into a wet ball.

"Hello, Mark."

"Hello, Mark," Roach mimicked. "Don't hang around, all right? The smell lingers."

Tom kept his mouth shut.

Roach fired the wad of paper into a nearby waste paper basket and stalked away.

"Charming as always," Kate said.

"Yeah."

"How's Pamela?"

"Busy. She's in Seattle, getting ready to shoot another picture."

"Wonderful. I hope she wins the Oscar with this one. I lost fifty bucks on her the last time around."

Tom looked at her. "Who was betting against her?"

"No one you know," she laughed. "Okay, it was my brother-in-law."

"What's his address?"

Paisley passed them and went into the interview room, closing the door sharply behind him.

"That's your cue," Tom said.

She nodded.

"A word with you afterward," he said.

She nodded again, closing the door on him.

CHAPTER 16

Tom was in the waiting area, reading more bulletins and public notices, when Paisley walked in with Kenneth Napier in tow.

"They won't let me film," Napier said. "I was going to bring in my camera, but they said no. Maybe they'll let me have some of their video later."

Tom looked at Paisley, who rolled his eyes. "Next."

Leonard was still in the interview room, writing in his notebook. Tom took the hot seat and crossed his legs as Paisley closed the door, not quite as sharply this time, and leaned back against it.

"Mister Faust," Leonard said, not looking up, "just a few questions and then you can take your charge back to wherever it is you're stashing him."

"Which is where?" Paisley asked.

Tom grunted. "Nice try."

Leonard glanced up. "Explain the connection between yourself and Mister Napier."

"Sure. I work for the Cage Intelligence Group, Toronto, and I've been assigned to oversee the protection of Mister Napier during your investigation of the Dessler homicide."

"Explain the connection between Cage Intelligence and Mister Napier. Is he considered an asset of some kind?"

"You mean an intelligence asset?"

Leonard waited.

Tom snorted. "That's above my pay grade. But I'd be surprised."

"So, what's the connection? Why is Cage Intelligence providing some mutt filmmaker with personal protection in connection to our homicide investigation?"

"You'll have to ask someone else that question, because I'm just doing the job that's been assigned to me."

"Should I ask Natalie Stone? Is she the one who gives you your assignments?"

"Yes, she is, and I don't really care whether you ask her questions or not. That's up to you and Detective Inspector Greene."

"Friends in high places? Is that what this is about?"

Tom said nothing.

Paisley stirred. "Did you know the victim before his death?"

Tom shook his head. "Total stranger."

"No prior connections at all?"

"Asked and answered, son."

"Do you think there's a connection between the homicide and the threats received by Mister Napier?"

"Pretty obvious, don't you think?"

Paisley bridled. "Nothing's obvious, Mister Faust. You of all people should know that."

There it was. The resentment lying below this bob-and-feint exercise. Tom was a retired detective inspector with a glowing personnel jacket and more than a little condescension in his attitude, and they didn't like it at all.

Tom stood up. "If there's nothing more."

"Stay where we can reach you."

In the corridor, Kate was back in her doorway. "I wish you wouldn't antagonize them like that."

"It's my job," Tom said. "I'm a prick."

She sighed, handing him a business card. "Call them if you learn something. Call *me* if it's something important."

Tom tucked the card into his shirt pocket and took out one of his own. "I've got an idea. Do you think you'd be interested in a little stint as a technical advisor for Pamela while she's doing this project in Seattle?" He wrote Pamela's number on the back of the card and gave it to her.

"Technical advisor?" She frowned at him.

"Look, this is unconnected to Dessler. Just something personal between you and me. Pammy's playing a Seattle ex-cop whose girl's kidnapped. She's on the outs with the department and goes after her daughter on her own. She'd be pleased to get them to bring you on as an advisor. They'll be shooting in October. You could apply for permission now and book some leave to fly out to Seattle when Pamela sends you her schedule. They'll cover all your expenses, I'm sure."

"Good lord, Tom."

"Yeah, I know. Anyway, think about it."

He patted her arm. "Gotta run. Otherwise the sons a bitches'll leave me here and I'll have to walk back."

CHAPTER 17

Norwood sat in a lawn chair outside the cabin, reading another of his magazines. This one was a back issue of *Fine Woodworking*: "back" meaning it had been published back in 1987. He had a run of them, and this particular issue had an article in it about tuning hand planes that he'd never read before and was finding quite interesting.

Norwood had a small collection of planes that he'd picked up here and there along the way, at yard sales or in second-hand stores, and while he liked the look and feel of them, he didn't use them very often, preferring the convenience of an electric plane. He kept them at home in Renfrew, in his workshop in the barn. He thought about them from time to time, and always kept his eye open for more to add to the collection. When he saw this article about tuning them so that they'd perform well, if he wanted to revert to a more handmade approach, he promised himself he'd try it out on a few of the best ones next time he went home to Renfrew.

Inside the cabin, the banging noises were still going on. After he finished the article, he'd go back inside to continue his work.

Tuning a plane involved several steps. First you took it apart and cleaned all the parts, removing rust if necessary. Then you sharpened the blade, made sure the bottom, called the sole, was flat, smooth, and clean, then you put it back together. Next you adjusted the height of the blade and its lateral angle, almost like checking the roll of an airplane, so that it was level and one side of the blade wasn't cutting deeper than the other side. After a series of other adjustments, the plane would be ready for use.

He jumped a little in the lawn chair when a scream ripped out through the half-open window. It had caught him off-guard, absorbed as he was in the article, but it didn't particularly worry him.

The motel whose cabin he was using was located on Highway 10 between Brampton and Caledon. It had been abandoned at some point in the 1990s, but Norwood had arranged through an alias about 10 years ago for the power to be turned back on. It was on a well-and-septic system, so having hydro ensured the water pump worked when Norwood wanted to use the place.

He liked this location for what he thought of as drastic interrogation work because of its isolation and all-around shabbiness. He liked to make sure his charges were conscious and aware of their surroundings when he marched them from the van into the cabin of his choice for the day, because he wanted them to think about how horrible and terrifying their situation was. He wanted them to realize that no help was coming. No one knew where they were. It was just them and Norwood.

One other cabin had seen previous use, the one down at the far end of the row, and that particular body was buried in the woods out back. At first, he was just going to leave it outside on the ground for the bears and coyotes to scavenge, but a scenario arose in his head whereby the scattered bones were found by random hikers who turned them in to the police, who ran DNA tests and connected a missing person to the area of Norwood's motel, and then . . .

It was worth the extra labour to dig the hole, bury the body, and put a log or something over the dirt to disguise the grave and keep the animals from digging it up.

Now Kendrick was weeping. With a sigh, Norwood put down the magazine and went back inside.

"I've told you what you want to know. Why are you doing this to me?"

Kendrick sat in a chair in the middle of the room. The old motel furniture, including the bed, side tables, lamps, and other junk had been thrown outside behind the cabin where they couldn't be seen from the road. Only the dresser remained, with its large mirror. Norwood had positioned the chair in front of the mirror so Kendrick could see himself at all times.

He was naked. His hands were tied behind the chair. His ankles were also bound, and his feet rested in a pan of water. Prominently displayed on the dresser were a car battery and jumper cables. Just for show, really. No doubt Kendrick had seen television programs where the pinchers were attached to some guy's nipples and then to the battery posts, creating a hell of a ruckus, but Norwood seldom bothered with technology. He just wanted Kendrick's imagination to run wild.

Norwood picked up his flayer, a six-inch filleting knife that he'd bought a few years ago in a kitchenware store in Vancouver during a job. It was Japanese, stainless steel, and razor-sharp. He'd already used it to inflict several cuts on Kendrick's face, torso, and thighs, close enough to the genitals without touching them that his victim could easily imagine the next step.

And avoiding the eyes, so that Kendrick could clearly see

himself in the mirror, see the blood running down his cheeks and dripping off his chin, et cetera et cetera.

Fairly early in the process, Kendrick had blurted out a location, his handsome features distorted in pain and fear. Duly noted. However, Norwood was a cautious man, and Kendrick had a lot of string left to play out before he croaked, so Norwood affected disbelief and kept going.

About ten more times, in ten minute intervals, he asked Kendrick for Napier's whereabouts. He was waiting for a different answer, the truth this time or maybe a misdirection, but the man remained consistent. Oxtongue Lake. Robertson Lane. Oxtongue Lake.

Bored and irritated that Kendrick wasn't making more of a challenge, he'd broken his nose with the heel of his fist and went outside to his magazine. He didn't want him to be breathing as easily as he was. Anyway, it was all part of the downward slide toward the inevitable end of the game.

Now, flayer in hand, he asked the question one more time and received the same sobbing answer. Oxtongue Lake.

All right, then. Fine. Mission accomplished.

Norwood put down the flayer and picked up a different knife, his Ka-Bar U.S. Marine Corps knife, just over seven inches long. A thicker and broader tool than the Jap blade.

He strolled behind Kendrick, chattering nonsense, and cut the man's throat from behind.

CHAPTER 18

Tom was drawn to Ariella Cohen's comm room by the persistent sound of a chime coming from one of her laptops.

Shortly after her arrival at the resort, she'd set up a surveillance network in one of the spare bedrooms. Tom had watched her crawl up onto the roof to install a small dish and what he thought was a radar array. She'd attached the latter, a slim box about the size of a cellphone, to the pole supporting the TV satellite dish and had used a hand drill to screw the former onto the roof on the other side.

Meanwhile, Bradley had established a perimeter around the resort with motion sensors, trail cameras, and other gear. Tom didn't know anything about any of it, but Bradley and Cohen seemed fully absorbed in their tasks and quite satisfied when everything seemed to be working the way it was supposed to work.

Now, they had a hit on something. Cohen was murmuring into her headset, feeding information to Bradley while she moved her mouse around, clicking on things and reading the output.

"Can you turn off the chime?" Tom asked.

Without replying, Cohen called up another window and killed the noise.

"Thanks. What have you got?"

"Movement. Multiple signals."

"Where?"

"About forty meters into the woods behind the cottage."

"Direction?"

"Lateral to our current position. Where's Napier?"

"In the kitchen. Writing."

Cohen nodded, then raised a hand to her headset and listened. "Roger. Want me to raise a drone?" She listened. "Copy that."

Over her shoulder, without taking her eyes off the screen, she said, "He's found a trail. Stand by."

"Does he need a drone?"

"Negative."

They waited.

Cohen stirred. "Copy that. Are you coming in?" She listened. "Roger that."

She removed the headset and slowly spun her chair around. "White-tailed deer. A small family of them, following the trail."

"I guess we can all stand down."

She grinned. "Yep."

Tom left, thinking that at least the technology was working properly. He was never one to mind a false alarm, as long as the system producing it was a reasonable safeguard to have in place if something more serious reared its head.

In the kitchen, Napier was leaning back in his chair, stretching his arms behind his head. "What was the noise?"

"Motion sensors. False alarm. Deer."

Napier stood up. "I need a break." He abruptly dropped his

pants, revealing swimming trunks. "Time for a dip. Coming?"

Napier led the way out onto the dock. He peeled off his shirt, draped it over one of the chairs, and dove in. Tom dropped into the other chair and watched him stroke, slowly and leisurely, out toward the middle of the lake.

After a few minutes, Elaine appeared with a cup of coffee for Tom, a tumbler of whisky for Napier, and a folded beach towel and bath robe, which she left on his chair.

Tom sipped his coffee. "This is very good, Elaine. What kind is it?"

"I don't know. I didn't look. Someone sent a box of it when Mister Napier first got here."

"Judd Kendrick?" Tom sipped again.

"I'm not sure. Sorry." She went back into the cottage.

Tom savoured the coffee while he kept an eye on Napier, who'd turned around and was slowly heading back. It was definitely the coffee he'd been served at Kendrick's office. This time, he was going to find out exactly what it was and where to get it.

Coffee had become a very important substitute for alcohol in Tom's life. He'd developed the habit of answering the frequent cravings for a drink with a cup of coffee, and it worked. He'd become an alcoholic who doesn't drink, and a coffee addict who was usually able to keep his new habit down to five or six cups a day. It was a good deal, as far as he was concerned.

Napier climbed back up onto the dock, shivering. "Christ, that's cold." He towelled himself off and threw on the robe. A pair of sunglasses followed, and then he made himself comfortable in the big chair.

Tom couldn't tell whether his eyes were open or closed, but he didn't particularly care. "Tell me more about this book you're writing. Why does somebody want to stop you from publishing it?"

Napier threw an arm over his head. "I don't know. It's just a book."

"Your life story."

"Yeah. Big deal, eh?"

"Academy Award winner. Sort of a big deal."

Napier finger-combed his tawny hair straight back. Wet, it was more brown than blond. "How I got into film. What kind of kid I was. How people don't know where the hell they're going to go with their life until suddenly they do."

Tom drank coffee.

"For me it happened early. Pretty much by chance."

"Tell me about it," Tom invited.

"I'm from Renfrew. Born and raised there, went to school there. How much do you know about it?"

"A bit. Under ten thousand population. Close to the Quebec border; an hour east of Ottawa; policed by the OPP. Been there a couple of times, but not often. They're Upper Ottawa Valley detachment, which is East Region. I worked Central."

"There you go, then. My hometown in a nutshell."

He sipped his whisky. Tom sipped his coffee, hoping Elaine would appear with more.

"My dad was a funeral director. He owned the biggest funeral home in the area. Started out as a mortician and bought the place when the old owner, Frederick Stanley, retired. It's still called the Stanley Funeral Home today. Dad never bothered to change the name. Even back then, people understood the value of brand awareness."

Tom listened.

"I grew up around dead bodies. It was no big deal to me. So

I'm not really afraid of death, like a lot of people are. It's just a phase, is how I see it. I believe that pop meme that may or may not have started with C.S. Lewis: 'you're not a body with a soul; you're a soul in a body.'"

Tom grunted.

"Anyway, I'd dress up sometimes and sit at the back during the services. It meant something to me, even though I'm not a practising Christian today. The words were always the same and the music was always the same and the people were always the same, either crying their eyes out or looking stiff and solemn. It was the ritual of it all that fascinated me. I'm still interested in ritual, but not in a religious sense. In a social sense. The things you might see in a Legion, for example, or a restaurant, or in a sports arena. Everywhere and anywhere, really. And don't get me started on ritual in filmmaking. We're the worst."

He drained his glass and looked over his shoulder, hoping to see Elaine trooping down from the cottage with refills. No joy.

"I enjoyed writing the chapter on how I first got started with film. It took me back. Happier times."

Elaine suddenly appeared, served their refills, and handed Tom a small empty bag. He turned it over and looked at the logo: Gold Seal Coffee. It was burlap, with information stamped on it in blue ink: Sumatra Mandhelling; fire roasted; hand crafted; artisan prepared; Prod. of Indonesia.

"That's what it is," she said.

"You like it?" Napier asked. "Judd sent it down to me. It's good."

"It's very good. May I keep this?" When Elaine nodded, he shoved it in his pocket. When she left, he looked at Napier. "You were going to tell me how you got started."

Napier slurped. "Yeah. Okay. When I was eleven, my best friend Dave Rogers got a Super 8 camera for his birthday. God, he was a good guy. His dad died in a plane crash overseas, but he was related to the you-know-who Rogers family, so he and his mom were well off. We were close for a while.

"An uncle sent him the camera but he wasn't really interested in it. I thought it might be fun to fool around with, so I traded him my baseball glove and a ball autographed by Gary Carter. He told his mom, so it wasn't a big deal, and she didn't make a fuss. His stuff was his to do with as he wished.

"I showed the camera to my dad, and the first thing he said was never to use it around the funeral home. Ever. So, I promised I wouldn't. Once we had that all cleared up and out of the way, he took me downtown to Darling's Camera Store and we talked to the owner, Tony Darling, a friend of his.

"The guy explained that Super 8 was a format for home movies and the camera would have cost a lot of money to buy, being nearly new. He found me an extra booklet that went with the model and sold me a cartridge of 8mm film that I could get developed when I used it up."

He smiled. "I was hooked right away. I dicked around with that first cartridge, shooting stuff at random, and when it was done Mister Darling developed it for me and sold me another cartridge. He also sold me a battered old projector he had in his back room, which I paid for in weekly installments from my allowance. He told me I had a good eye, and that this time I should write a little storyboard and shoot a real movie."

He drained his glass and set it down by his foot.

"This was Grade Six. I wasn't much of a writer, but a friend of mine in class, Sally Norwood, was pretty good. She was already writing short stories and stuff, and the teachers were all impressed. So I convinced her to help me on a weekend project.

"We went to the library and found some books. I remember them so clearly, because I couldn't make heads nor tails of them at the time but she devoured them all. *The Filmmaker's Handbook* by Ascher and Pincus; *How to Write a Movie in 21 Days* by Viki King; and she even tackled William Goldman's *Adventures in the Screen Trade*. She was a genius. I was in awe of her."

"What happened to her? Did she get into the business too?"

Napier stared off across the lake. "She disappeared. That summer, 1989. She was never found."

"I'm sorry to hear that. Runaway?"

He made a noise. "No. Of course not. She was popular in school; her parents were good; her brother was a bit of a dickhead, but that didn't make any difference." He sighed. "That's another reason I remember those books so well. I stopped by on my bike to pick her up, but she wasn't there. Her brother was the only one home. He said he didn't know where she was. Her library books were sitting on a chair on the verandah, like she'd put them down while she went for her bike, but that was it. The only trace of her. I rode by the next week and the books were still sitting there, so I took them back to the library for her."

"Nothing turned up in the search?"

"Nothing. It was heart-breaking. I didn't touch the camera for nearly two months, but then I realized I *had* to make films. I owed it to her. So that's what I did."

His shivering had stopped. He ran his fingers through his hair again. It was starting to dry out. "Here I am telling you my life story for free, when I should make you wait and pay for the book."

"I'm not much of a reader."

"When I finished high school," Napier went on, obviously a talker once he got started on a subject, "I went out to Simon Fraser and did my film studies degree out there. I have to admit, by that time Sally was just a memory and I was doing it for myself. Just so the record's straight."

"Fine."

"After I graduated, I stayed out there. Vancouver was now Hollywood North, so there was lots of work. Television, features, you name it. I made a decent living for six years dressing sets and plugging and unplugging stuff, shooting my own footage on the side, trying to put ideas together into a project. I did a couple of shorts that were junk; then I shot something called *Heavy Duty*, about a guy at the Vancouver Zoo who looked after the hippos."

He laughed. "Fun stuff. I submitted it to the York University Film Festival and won first prize. That was in oh-eight. Talk about a shock. I got some expressions of interest from producers; I flew to Toronto for meetings; I hired an agent to help me pitch my next project; moved to Toronto; fired the agent; made the next short, which was about an old Irish guy who sold pencils on Yonge Street; handled my own legal stuff and distribution agreements; then I just kept making films. Graduated from shorts to documentary features; started connecting with investors and crew members, and it all just grew from there."

"Make any enemies along the way?"

This time Napier's laugh was without humour. "Sure. Plenty, I guess. It's a competitive business."

"A college nemesis jealous of your accomplishments?"

"A couple of guys at Simon Fraser I didn't get along with.

One's dead, and the other's in New Zealand working on another blockbuster fantasy film. I think he's probably forgotten all about me."

"People you've fired? Someone you've clashed with, an investor or maybe a rival for the Oscar?"

"Look Tom, a lot of people don't like me. I'm aggressive; I rub them the wrong way. I get what I want, when I want it, and I never, ever apologize for it. There are a lot of wacky people in the business, some of them"—he pointed at his head and drew circles in the air—"but I would be truly surprised if any of them, any that I know, would resort to death threats and homicide. It just doesn't make sense. There's hate, and then there's homicide. Two different things, as I see it."

"I think we have to consider all the possibilities at this point."

CHAPTER 19

As a carpenter, Norwood had his favourite tools. His favourite hammer, his favourite power drill, his favourite measuring tape. He always reached for them first, believing that his work was that much better because of the tool.

As a professional assassin, he also had his favourite tools. His favourite knife, his favourite garrotte, and yes, his favourite drone.

His knife, which he often used for assassinations overseas, was the original World War II Ka-Bar USMC Red Spacer knife, with a blade length of just over seven inches and a perfect balance in his hand, that he'd used to end Judd Hendrick's brief stay on earth. He always made sure the knife was well-wrapped in his checked luggage, and he'd never experienced difficulty travelling with it.

He had seven garrottes in his collection and was always on the lookout for more. His favourite was also vintage World War II but had been hand-made by someone who'd spent time ensuring that the wooden handles felt comfortable to grip. The initials H. and G. had been carved into the handle butts. The ligature was piano wire, thin and deadly. He'd used it once, shortly after acquiring it in Brazil, and it performed spectacularly. It stayed in his collection after that, and he tended to rotate the others into service whenever he brought one with him on a job.

As for the drone, his favourite was now in the air above the Oxtongue Lake resort where Kenny Napier was hiding out. It was a high-end military surveillance drone capable of an altitude of 4,000 meters. It had a battery charge time of 90 minutes and a range of eight kilometers. It had high-resolution video and photo cameras; a thermal camera, and a night mode camera. It came with GPS tracking and pin-fly controls where you could set GPS points on your phone and the drone would follow the flight path completely hands-free. It also had a follow feature, where you could instruct the drone to follow you anywhere you moved, whether on foot or in a vehicle. It had cost him several thousand bucks USD, but it was well worth it.

The beauty of a pre-programmed pin flight, which he had the drone running on right now, was that it was controlled by an Android app that couldn't be intercepted by RF detectors. Most drones are controlled by radio signals that not only enable the user to manipulate the drone in flight, but also to receive video, position, remaining battery power, and other information.

A radio frequency detector can intercept these signals, identify the drone, and even provide the location of the operator. None of which was a very good thing to have happen if you're trying to conduct covert surveillance on a target.

Norwood had programmed a flight path that would take the drone around the perimeter of the resort several times, then conduct multiple fly-overs to view the property from various angles. He was also making several passes using the thermal camera to find out how many people were there and what they might be doing.

It was all great fun. He was parked in a driveway leading into the bush, someone's hunting camp trail or something, five kilometers away from the lake. He watched the video display idly, in case something outlandish popped up below, but he wasn't worried about details right now because he'd subject the video and still images to intense scrutiny a bit later.

Eventually, the drone lost altitude, made a final run over the resort, and then completed its program, landing lightly and efficiently on the road not three meters from where Norwood stood. He loaded it into his van and drove to Bracebridge, where he took a motel room under one of his aliases, had a pizza delivered, and settled down with a notebook and pen to study what his favourite drone had brought back for him.

CHAPTER 20

Tom sat in a chair outside the comm room, eating one of Elaine's Reuben sandwiches and reading the news feed on his cellphone. He was looking for an update on the Dessler investigation, but nothing new had been published so far today.

He figured the detectives would still be working their way through Dessler's client list, while others would be combing his e-mail, texts, and social media for red flags. Time-consuming work, and boring at times, but necessary. Who knew if it would produce any tangible leads? More likely just eye strain and a few nagging migraines.

He finished the sandwich, wiped his hands, and set his plate on the arm of the chair. As he did so, he heard Cohen stirring.

"Bradley, what's your twenty?"

She was using a push-to-talk phone, which allowed Tom to hear both sides of the conversation.

"Driveway. All clear."

"I've got something you should see."

"There in two."

Tom got up and stood in the doorway. "What is it?"

Eyes on her monitors, she didn't reply.

He wandered over to a chair and sat down.

Bradley bustled in. "What is it?"

"Here. Look. Picked this up on radar." She played him a recording.

"Twelve minutes ago," he said, leaning forward to read the display. "South-southwest to north-northeast. Gone in seven, no, nine seconds."

He looked at her. "Bird?"

"Unlikely. I think it was a drone."

Bradley frowned. "RF?"

"Zip. If it was a drone, it was computer-controlled. No radio whatsoever."

"Could it have been a cottager?" Tom asked. "A kid, fooling around with one?"

Bradley ignored him. "Log it," he told Cohen. He turned to leave the room.

Tom stood up. "What about a bird? A duck or a cormorant?"

Bradley went through the door. Tom followed him.

"Are you going to follow up on it? See if someone in the area was playing with a drone? What if it wasn't? What if it was surveillance?"

Bradley turned on him. "Look, if you want to jump in your rent-a-car and drive around the lake to waste your time on door-to-door interviews, be my guest. But you'll leave us a body short while you're gone." He poked Tom in the chest. "My advice, Faust? Forget about it. Leave the surveillance to the professionals."

Tom bridled. "Listen, mister. There's a chain of command here, and I'm at the top of it. Have you got that?"

Bradley walked away.

CHAPTER 21

Although it was evening, Tom obeyed his craving and made himself a strong pot of coffee, hoping that the caffeine wouldn't keep him up all night.

Cup in hand, he went into the great room, where Napier was watching television.

"Baseball fan?" He made himself comfortable in a leather armchair.

"Blue Jays fan. I've got season's tickets, but I never seem to be able to make it to the games. My EA's in charge of making sure they get dispensed to people I need to keep interested in me."

Tom didn't think that Napier had mentioned his executive assistant before. "What's her name?"

"His name. Chase Roblin. Nice guy. Wants to produce someday."

"It's my understanding you haven't married."

Napier took his eyes off the screen to give him a thin smile. "Trope Number Sixteen: married to his work. Trope Number Seventeen: nope, not gay."

"So no vengeful ex out there willing to pay the big bucks to have you shot in the neck with a crossbow bolt?"

"No," Napier grimaced. "Is that really how he died?"

Tom nodded. "Weapon of opportunity, but the guy's a pro."

"Lovely. I've got my very own personal Crossbow Killer after me."

With Napier's agent on his mind, Tom's thoughts moved laterally. "You said you filmed Dessler at some point after he received the threat from this guy."

"Yeah."

"That's something I'd like to see."

Napier was watching the screen as a Blue Jays player trotted around the bases after hitting a home run. The crowd cheered wildly; Napier was smiling. "What?"

"I said I'd like to see the video of Dessler's interview."

"Dessler? Sure. It's on the laptop."

"Think I could watch it now?"

"Now?" He glanced at the TV. "I'll bring it in."

Tom drank his coffee, thinking. It was possible Dessler had said something about the threat that hadn't been picked up on by Napier but that might jump out at Tom, who was trained and experienced in such things. If that were the case, the video would have to be forwarded to Kate Greene and her detectives.

Napier came in and set up his laptop on the coffee table where Tom could see it.

"What else you got on here, Ken?"

"A bunch of stuff. Notes; drafts; video clips; a couple of my short docs. A lot of stuff I shot in college and when I was a kid."

Using the track pad, Napier navigated to a menu and glanced at Tom.

"Enter the time machine," he said.

"Pardon me?"

Napier's smile was faint. "The time machine. It's my own little pet philosophy. Film as a time machine."

"I'm afraid I don't understand."

"Think of all the science fiction stories about time travel, where someone goes back to witness life that has fallen behind us on the time stream. *The Time Traders* by Andre Norton. They go on an operation to the Bronze Age and insert themselves into a group of Beaker people in Britain. Or the great Harlan Ellison *Star Trek* episode, "The City on the Edge of Forever," where Kirk goes back to pre-war America to find McCoy, who's undergoing a fit of temporary insanity. Remember that one? He lets Edith Keeler die so she won't alter history. Those are fiction, though. Mine are fact."

He paused, rubbing his eyes. "Just one example. *Yonge Street Graphite Blues*. I shot that with just one camera. Tommy Grant, born in Belfast in 1934, came to Canada as a young longshoreman. Worked on the waterfront for quite a while, but alcohol gradually destroyed him, as it does so many others. Ended up selling pencils on Yonge Street outside a peep show theatre."

"Mmm."

"I passed him on the sidewalk every day for nearly a week before I brought my gear and got his consent to film him. He took me to the room he lived in, showed me his few belongings, photographs from home, a pocket watch that belonged to his grandfather, stuff like that. It made a hell of a short. One of my favourites."

He looked at Tom. "He's dead, now. He died of exposure the next winter. He fell asleep on the sidewalk and a snow plow buried him. But you can watch *Graphite Blues* and go back in time and see him when he was still a living, breathing human being with memories, regrets, a sense of humour, everything that makes us who we are while we're alive. That's why I do what I do. To film the present before it becomes the past."

He clicked on a file. It took a moment to load, and then it began to play. He sat down, muted the volume on the television, and watched the ball game without sound as Tom leaned forward, pulling out his notebook and pen.

Irwin Dessler was a small man. He sat in a wooden chair, legs planted firmly on the floor, his attention slightly off-camera as he spoke to Napier. His head looked larger than it should have been, mostly because of his untidy mop of wavy, grey hair combed up off his forehead. It made him look like a nineteenth-century poet or painter, brilliant and more than a little eccentric.

"I can forward it to the part where he talks about the threat," Napier said.

"This is fine."

The interview began. "How did you get into the business, Win?" Napier asked, off-screen.

"Ah, the old origin story. Got an hour?"

"We've got as long as you want."

"All right." He crossed his legs and folded his hands on his knees. His brown tweed trousers were cuffed. Under his suit jacket, his pale yellow shirt was open at the neck.

"I grew up in Milton, which I suppose is a good place for a literary agent to be from, since it actually *was* named after the poet. My dad drove a taxi in town and my mom took in laundry, so there wasn't a lot of money, but it was okay. No complaints.

"I did all right in school, but nothing spectacular. Middle of the pack. My grades in English were good, though. You asked me how I got into the business, and in truth the answer is a combination of things, but there was one thing in particular when I was in high school—Grade Ten, I think—that gave me a big shove in the right direction."

He uncrossed his legs and shifted in the chair, trying to get more comfortable.

"What was that, Win?"

"We lived in a poorer part of town. There were train tracks that cut across the neighbourhood, a CP line, if I remember correctly. Freight trains. When I was in high school, as I say, there was a man, a homeless man, who lived under one of the train bridges. Maybe in his forties? Scraggly beard and long hair. Always wore a full-length grey coat and liked to hang out in the reading room of the Milton public library. I remember very clearly how he smelled. I can still smell it, when I think about it. And you could still smell it in the room after the library staff asked him to leave. You knew when he'd been in there, reading a book.

"But he never caused trouble. He was very quiet and respectful of others. He just wanted some place warm and dry to sit and read a book."

Dessler cleared his throat. "Excuse me."

"Do you want some water?"

"No, thanks. I'm fine. This Saturday I'm trying to tell you about, I went to the library in the morning for a biology assignment I was working on. This man—his name turned out to be Walter Redding—was standing outside handing out pieces of paper. Unusual for him. I took one. It was a sheet of yellow lined paper torn from a notepad. A poem was written on it. Handwritten, I mean. He'd done up about a dozen copies and was trying to hand them out to people, who mostly just avoided him. I folded the paper and put it in my pocket.

"'Read it,' he said. His voice was very low, a baritone, and a little rough.

" 'When I get home,' I promised.

"He nodded and turned away to somebody else, forgetting I was there.

"When I got home, I remembered the poem and took it out. I still have it somewhere, in my papers. I'm not sure where, but I kept it. I read it so many times I memorized it."

"What was it about, Win?"

Tom watched Dessler close his eyes and tip his head back, summoning the memory. Then he began to recite:

I Hate the Tyrant Gravity

by Walter Redding

> I hate the tyrant gravity;
> I hate its laws and I hate its regulations.
> It makes me lie down against my will;
> It causes me to grow old before my time.
> A constant weight around my neck,
> It pulls me down and down and down
> Until my back curves, my flesh sags,
> And my brittle bones splinter with old age.
> It causes things to drop and fall,
> So that I must always bend my aching back
> To pick them up again.
> Always something dropping;
> Always something fallen.
> I fear the day will surely come
> When I no longer have the strength
> to pick them up again.

The video was silent for a moment as Dessler sat there, eyes still closed.

"Wow," Napier said, off-screen.

"Yeah." Dessler opened his eyes. "Walter Redding disappeared from town not long after that. Not that I noticed; I went on with my life just like everybody else until a couple of months later I realized I hadn't seen him since that day at the library. I went for a walk along the train tracks. His stuff had all been cleared out from under the bridge, like he'd never been there. I don't know if he died or just caught a train to try his luck somewhere else."

"It must have had a powerful impact," Napier said, "if it's stuck with you all these years."

"It did."

"Tell me about the death threat you recently received."

Up to now, Tom had been taking a few cursory notes, writing down his impressions of the victim, including his demeanour, his non-verbals, and the way his mind seemed to work, mildly self-deprecating but at the same time firmly self-confident. The poem wasn't in itself important, as far as Tom was concerned, but it told him that Dessler not only had an excellent memory but a certain amount of empathy. What that meant to the price of salmon in Seattle Tom had no idea, but it was all grist for the mill at this point.

Now, however, Napier's abrupt change of subject brought Tom's eyes back up from the page. Just in time to catch a fleeting grimace that crossed Dessler's face as his eyes flicked to the left. An indication that he was recalling an auditory memory.

"He was using one of those voice distortion apps. You know, so you can't tell if it's a man or a woman, young or old, human or Martian. You hear them in the movies and you sort of get used to the concept, if you know what I mean, but to experience one on your own phone right out of the blue is creepy. It scared me right away. A shock ran through my whole body. Who is this, and what do they want from me?"

"I can't imagine."

Dessler smiled wanly. "No, you were spared the experience, Ken, because you've been incommunicado to the world. Fortunately. I, however. . ."

"What did they say?"

"They said, 'Is this Irwin Dessler?' 'Of course,' I said, 'you called my number, didn't you?' They didn't like the sarcasm, the attempt at bravery. They told me to shut my smart mouth and listen. So I did. They said, 'Kenny Napier is writing a book. Stop him immediately and see that he destroys all his files and printouts. Everything.' "

Tom leaned forward and used the track pad to pause the video. "Is that the way the caller referred to you? 'Kenny'? Not 'Kenneth' or 'Ken'?"

Napier frowned. "I don't know. That's what Win said," he waved at the laptop, "and his memory was obviously very good, so I assumed he was quoting verbatim."

"Dessler called you 'Ken' a couple of times during the interview. Is that what he usually called you? Not 'Kenneth' or 'Kenny'?"

"I never really thought about it, but I suppose you're right. Some people use my full name, especially when we're doing business, and with other people it's just 'Ken.' No one calls me 'Kenny' anymore."

Tom wrote it down in his notebook, then resumed watching the video.

Dessler was shaking his head. "I told them there was nothing

I could do. You'd already signed a contract with the publisher, and it was out of my hands. They didn't like that at all. They wanted to know what the hell I was good for if I couldn't tell the publisher the deal was off.

"I said it wasn't that simple, you can't just cancel a contract unilaterally for no good reason. That's not how it works. I said, 'You obviously don't know anything about contracts.'

"They said, 'Yeah, I do. All right. Where's Napier now?' I said I didn't know, his manager was looking after all that. I was pretty much out of the picture. Then they said, 'If I find out you've been lying to me, you're going to die a slow and painful death. I'm serious. Deadly serious.' Then they just, well, hung up."

Tom watched the video for another few minutes, but nothing else of interest presented itself, so he finished his notes and closed the lid on the laptop. Napier came over and gathered it up.

"Find anything?"

"Not really. The name thing bothers me, though. 'Kenny.' Sounds like someone who knew you in the past."

"Sounds pretty trivial, if you ask me." He left the room, laptop under his arm.

You'd be damned surprised, Tom thought, where trivial stuff can sometimes lead you.

CHAPTER 22

Norwood was stretched out on his bed, on top of the covers, propped up on two hard pillows, his laptop balanced on top of his stomach.

The television was on, the volume turned up just loud enough so that the couple in the next room could hear it and think he was another weary traveller, dosing himself to sleep with crap programming.

He was working. He preferred to work on the laptop rather than a cellphone, because the encryption was better, the screen was larger, and he had all his best communications tools here.

Right now he was using a special browser to navigate the darknet, where he carried out most of his transactions. A private underground network, the darknet was highly encrypted and could only be accessed by using software not available to the regular crowd. His browser, for example, didn't have a name. It was identified by a collection of random characters and symbols. It carried him to the portals of applications so private only a few select users were able to log in.

Norwood's alias for the website he was currently working in was Angus Black. His avatar was a head-and-shoulders photo of a young man with long black hair, thick eyebrows, and a hard stare. He'd swiped it from some kid's Facebook account after he died. No one reported the death to the social media company or did anything about it, so the account remained open and accessible. The photo suited Norwood's purposes because the young man had had very few friends, and no one had commented on his last several posts, which were three years old when Norwood came across him.

He preferred an actual photo instead of a cartoon or animal picture or the like because he wanted to put an image of a real person in the minds of the individuals he dealt with down here. Involuntarily, they'd associate him with a long-haired young man, maybe a Billy the Kid or someone like that. His actual appearance would remain a mystery that no one would bother to try to solve.

Right now he was chatting with an entity named Devoir. Norwood received his assignments from a couple of sources, but he preferred to work with Devoir, who was completely reliable. Not to say trustworthy; no one could be trusted in the world in which Norwood moved. Reliable, though. Predictable. Consistent.

Norwood had looked up the word "devoir" once and saw that it translated from the French as "duty, obligation, mission." Devoir's avatar was a stylized photo of a man's hand, fingers long and bony, holding a small metal skull. It struck Norwood as a bit over the top, but then he thought it might be another piece of misdirection, similar to his own.

Norwood was asking Devoir to set up a new assignment for him that would start in four or five days. It was rare for Norwood to initiate contact this way, and slightly against his community's etiquette. Devoir was fine with it, however, and was giving it his consideration.

I have something coming up in Belize. Completion date is ten days from now, but you could go down there early.

Belize. He'd never been there before, although he'd been in neighbouring Guatemala once on a job early in his career.

What's it pay?

One million. USD.

I'll take it.

The target is a politician. There'll be security.

The extra days will help the recon. I'll take it.

It's yours. The packet will reach you by midnight your time.

The packet being a physical delivery of photos, information, cash, and the coordinates of a local contact in Belize who would supply him with whatever he asked for.

Send it to my address in 18 hrs.

Will do.

That was it. His backdoor would be all set up for him to disappear through as soon as this personal thing was cleared off the board.

Eighteen hours should do it.

CHAPTER 23

Tom was still in the great room, sprawled in the leather armchair. Napier was in the kitchen, talking to Elaine. Cohen was napping, and Bradley was lurking somewhere, doing Protection Guy stuff, presumably.

Tom had his ear buds in, listening to music. Right now it was a West German progressive rock band from the 1970s called Grobschnitt. The album was called *Rockpommel's Land*, released in 1977. Their stuff was very reminiscent of early Genesis, and he was enjoying it when Cliff Bruckner came in and sat down on the couch.

Tom tried to ignore him, but the old man obviously wanted to talk, so Tom shut off the music and pulled out his buds.

"What can I do for you, Cliff?"

"Sorry to interrupt your listening. Taylor Swift?"

Tom chuckled. "Not exactly. How's your knee?"

"Oh, it's better. Thanks for asking. Just limping a little bit now. Helluva bruise, though."

"That's what you get for trying to bushwhack a cop."

"Guess you're right, at that."

Cliff had arrived before dinner with a load of groceries

and supplies, including Napier's preferred bourbon, and after unloading his truck had decided to stay overnight. He left his truck at the back, just outside the rear kitchen door.

"What's on your mind?" Tom repeated.

"What's your take on all this death threat stuff, Faust? Do you take it seriously?"

"It's my job to take it seriously."

"I suppose. I thought it would be okay just to set up my trail camera in the driveway, but these two guys have gone the whole nine yards with their gear and procedures and all the rest of it."

"That's *their* job. Speaking of which, what did you say you do for a living?"

Cliff lifted a haunch and pulled out his wallet. He tweezered out a business card and, leaning forward, passed it over.

" 'Bruckner Charter Fishing,' " Tom read aloud. "Is that like taking rich people out to catch sailfish off the Florida Keys?"

"Sort of. Some great freshwater fishing in this area. You might be surprised."

Tom stuck the card in his wallet. It was an old detective's habit. When someone volunteered personal information, you hung onto it.

"I don't know the first thing about fishing."

"Takes years to get to know these lakes around here. I spent two hundred and fifty days a year on the water when I first started up. Built myself a chart of each lake, the fish in it, water temperatures three times a day year-round, currents, you name it. Ice fishing, too. I still update my info on a regular basis. This is serious business, and there's lots of money in it. I make a nice living."

Tom shrugged. "I've heard that a lot of celebrities have

places up here. Rock stars, athletes."

"Not on this lake, no, but on some of the others around here. My clients are more the corporate type, returning customers who make it a yearly vacation trip. Guys who want to loosen their ties for a week and have fun. No drinking, though. Not on my boats. Quickest way for me to lose my licence."

"But not celebrities?"

"They tend to make their own arrangements," Cliff said.

Napier wandered in, yawning. "Coffee break. I swiped some of yours, Tom. There's still some left. Anybody interested?"

"Not me," Cliff said, standing up. "Time for me to catch up on my beauty rest. I promised the landlord I'd finish chopping the leftover wood in the morning."

"I'll have whatever's left," Tom said. He waited for a moment to see if Napier would go back for it, then accepted the folly of the notion and stood up.

"Cops and their coffee, eh?" Napier said, his eyes back on the television.

"Something like that," Tom murmured.

CHAPTER 24

The following morning, Norwood checked out of his motel room and drove to Oxtongue Lake. As he drove, he admired the passing scenery. It must be a beautiful place in the fall, he thought. All the colours of the trees in the fall, the fresh air, apple orchards, and pumpkin fields and all the rest of it.

While eating his breakfast this morning, he'd looked up Belize on the Internet. Apparently it was getting close to the end of the dry season down there, and the temperature was anywhere from 25 degrees Celsius to 30 degrees. Which suited Norwood, since he loved warm weather and blue skies. And no tropical storms or other horseshit like that. A good time of the year to stalk and kill some worthless bastard. Correction: some million-dollar bastard.

As well, Belize didn't have an extradition treaty with Canada, which would be handy if they caught up to him at home and tried to nail him for the elimination of little Kenny Napier. He didn't like remaining in a country after he'd done a job, but as a last resort he could hole up there until the winds blew a little cooler in Canada. It was a contingency plan, anyway. One of several.

He called Sharon to explain that his schedule had changed and he wouldn't be home for another two weeks or so. His cover story with her was that he worked for the Department of National Defence as a civilian contractor, a carpenter working in the far north at one of the Arctic bases currently undergoing extensive renovations at taxpayers' expense. They were running behind schedule, and his part of the project had been delayed because they'd run out of concrete and had to send up more. Which chewed up valuable time. And cost some poor doorknob procurement manager his job along with it.

"I understand," she said.

Norwood knew she loved the money he put into their joint account at the end of each month. Over the years he'd proven his ability to take on high-risk assignments, and his fees had risen accordingly. A lot of the money ended up in offshore accounts, but a decent percentage went to Sharon and the three girls. It was his way of keeping her happy with their long-distance relationship.

The deposits were declared income from a fake account with a fake contracting company working for DND, amounting to about ten thousand a month after deductions. Sharon filed accurate income tax returns on it each year.

On the other hand, it was the packages of cash he couriered to her that she really liked. Another ten grand in used twenties, non-sequential, shipped every month at a cost of about $130. No explanation offered, and none asked for.

Sharon wasn't stupid. She understood that the taxation people often looked for people living a lifestyle more lavish than what their income should support, and she kept her spending smart and inconspicuous. What she did with the cash, he wasn't sure. He remembered reading a magazine article once about pilots who flew dope into the United States from the Caribbean and would hide their cash in coffee cans buried in the back yard. Wild stuff.

At the same time, Sharon never questioned his cover story, which gave her something to tell the girls, and she never complained about the absences. When he came home between assignments, she treated him right. The girls were always very excited.

Norwood was a happily married man who happened to kill people for a living.

Halfway up the lane to the resort, there was a gated entrance to an ATV trail used in the winter by hunters. It was similar to the setup he'd used before, five kilometers from here, while surveilling the place.

This spot gave him enough room to pull over and set up shop. He programmed a quick run that sent his drone straight up 500 feet and circled several times above the cottage. He used the thermal camera and, watching the display, saw four bodies inside and two outside. Three of the four inside were grouped together in what Norwood figured would be the kitchen, where they'd be enjoying a leisurely breakfast, while the fourth was off on their own. Bathroom.

One body outside was at the side of the cottage, making small movements back and forth. Some kind of work, no doubt. Listening, Norwood heard the faint sound of wood being chopped. Okay, fine. The other body was in the woods behind the resort. Perimeter Man.

Norwood brought the drone back and put it away. He changed into camouflage, combat boots, and black Mechanix-wear gloves. The gloves were made of goatskin leather, were flame-resistant, and had amazing tactile feel. They had cost him more than $200, and they went with him on every assignment.

He covered his face with three-colour camouflage paint, strapped his trusty Ka-Bar knife to his thigh, and slipped the garrotte into a leather pouch on his belt. Activating a device that would disrupt any perimeter sensors around the place, he left the vehicle and cut through the trees to circle the cottage.

Detecting a faint sound, he stopped and crouched. After a few long moments he could hear someone approaching through the forest. Perimeter Man, no doubt.

He waited patiently, and eventually was rewarded with movement on his ten o'clock. Unlike Perimeter Man, Norwood was an expert in silent approach, having staked his life on perfect technique quite a few times before. He slowly crept up on the man from behind, patiently closing the distance between them.

The man stopped.

Norwood stopped.

The man made some kind of crinkling sound. A candy wrapper, most likely.

Norwood moved forward. Ten meters. Five meters. Three.

The man slowly moved.

Norwood picked up his pace, readying the garrotte in his hands, and before the man knew what was happening, the piano wire had circled his neck from behind and his throat was neatly cut.

Norwood stepped back, watching the blood spurt as the man's legs turned to rubber and gravity slowly lowered him down to earth. Norwood stepped forward and looked at the man's face. His eyes were open and lifeless.

Norwood felt satisfaction. Killing didn't excite him, or give him a thrill, or any of that other perverted stuff. There was just satisfaction, the knowledge of being really good at something and carrying through on it successfully.

The dead man wore black coveralls with a stylized CIG logo on the front and "Cage Intelligence" at the bottom. Norwood quickly searched the body, confiscating a military-grade baton, a so-so knife with questionable balance, and a push-to-talk phone. Changing his mind on the knife, he tossed it into the woods and resumed his circumnavigation of the cottage.

He spotted a bush that had already begun to produce large green leaves. He grabbed a handful, ran the garrotte wire through them to clean it off, and threw them away.

The sound of wood being chopped grew louder. Norwood emerged from the trees on the far side of the building and saw an old man steadying a chunk of wood on a stump. As Norwood quickly covered the ground between them, the man chopped the chunk into two pieces. The blade of his axe stuck in the stump. He yanked at it. It didn't budge.

The garrotte went around his neck and did its work a second time.

Four to go. One of them, Kenny Napier.

On his hip, a red LED on the push-to-talk began to flash. He turned up the volume, listened to a woman's voice trying to raise Bradley—no doubt the stiff Norwood had left behind in the woods—and after a moment he killed the volume again. If Bradley was Mr. Outside, then this person would be Ms. Inside.

Norwood surveyed the cottage. He was a few meters from the dining room, an extension that was mostly windows and sliding French doors.

Four targets still inside. Step One would be to see which ones he could lure outside where his garrotte could add to its score. Easier than having to infiltrate and navigate through uncertain rooms and hallways. Step Two would then have to be an interior mop-up. Not his favourite thing: hide and seek.

He looked at the picture window closest to him. Through it he could see a long dining room table with a long bamboo runner and six chairs. He looked at the corpse of the old man and looked at the window again.

It gave him an idea.

CHAPTER 25

Tom was walking through the dining room on his way to the kitchen when something large crashed through the picture window and landed on the big table right in front of him. He raises his arm to shield his face from flying glass shards as the body of Cliff Bruckner careened across the table and over the edge onto the floor at his feet.

Cohen dashed into the room, shouting into her push-to-talk. A voice responded, yelling something fuzzy and inarticulate. It didn't sound like Bradley's voice.

She pointed at Tom. "Get down!"

He crouched next to Cliff's body.

She ran to the sliding French doors and pelted outside. Tom heard her boots thump on the cedar deck, followed by a dull thud as she jumped to the ground, and then silence.

Cliff's head had been nearly severed from his neck, the laceration so thin that it could only have been made by a garrotte. Although he'd seen several ligature strangulations over the course of his career, he'd never seen this kind outside of textbooks. It was extremely ugly.

He wheeled into the kitchen and grabbed Elaine, who was

coming out to see what was happening.

"Stay in here. No. In here."

She stared at him, but let him jostle her away from the dining room. Napier had risen from the kitchen table, a glass of orange juice smashed on the floor near his feet.

Tom suddenly remembered Cliff's truck, parked just outside the kitchen door. "Pack up your stuff!" he directed Napier. He pointed at Elaine. "Help him."

Crouching, Tom eased back into the dining room and went through Cliff's pockets, confiscating his keys and his wallet.

He paused for a moment. Silence. Then the soft snick of the front door opening.

He crab-walked back into the kitchen. Napier was zipping up his knapsack, looking scared. Elaine had removed her backpack from a hook inside the door and slung it over her shoulder.

"What about Grandpa? Is he still outside?"

So she hadn't been able to tell what was lying on the dining room floor. Tom was grateful for small mercies.

"Out the back door and into the truck when I say the word," Tom ordered.

"What about Grandpa?" Elaine repeated.

"He's gone. We'll talk about it later. We have to *move*."

"Come on," Napier said, grabbing her arm.

Tom took out the key fob for his rental car. It was parked near the front door, next to the Suburban. He pressed the remote start and heard the car engine burst into life.

"Go!"

Elaine led the way, opening the driver's side door and jumping up behind the wheel. Napier took the passenger side, dropping his knapsack on the floor between his feet.

Tom used his arm to prevent Elaine from shutting the door.

"Get over. I'm driving."

She squirmed over on the bench seat to give him room to get in. He shoved Cliff's key into the ignition, started up the truck, and floored it.

The back lane followed a narrow track through the forest. The trees were so close that branches whacked across the windshield. Beside him, Elaine whimpered.

Gritting his teeth, Tom kept the accelerator pinned to the floorboard, his hands gripping the steering wheel in a stranglehold. Thankfully, the truck had an automatic transmission. Not having to drive stick would be one less thing to divide his attention.

It was a 1984 Chevrolet Scottsdale. It had 179,556 on the odometer. In miles. It was a brown-and-yellow shitbox with rust around the tire wells and rocker panels disappearing into the ether in large flakes. The tailgate rattled with every bump, and junk in the back jumped up and down, making a noise like big metal beans in a coffee can.

Inside, there was miscellaneous litter in the footwells and a tear in the vinyl on the dash above the glove compartment. The cab smelled of oil and stale sweat and fish.

Finally, the lane connected to a road circling around the lake on the other side from the resort. Tom glanced in the rear-view mirror but couldn't see any sign of the assailant. They were raising a rooster-tail of dust behind them, but there was no tell-tale glint of running lights or the sun flashing off a windshield.

Had the distraction of remote-starting the rental car given them enough time to get away?

He checked the mirrors again. Nothing behind them.

Okay. So. Now then.

Where the hell were they going to go?

PART TWO

THE PURSUIT

Tom was relieved when they finally reached a county road that was paved and had shoulders wide enough to keep the trees at bay while they raced along, muffler roaring and springs creaking.

Beside him, Elaine sat on her hands, her backpack between her feet. Napier was bent over, fussing with his knapsack. He pulled out a hand-held video camera and, cranking down the window, leaned out and began to film the road behind them.

"Stop that!" Tom snapped.

Shrugging, Napier rolled up the window and filmed the road ahead of them through the windshield.

"Can't you take me home?" Elaine asked. "I want to go home."

Tom shook his head. "Not a good idea right now."

He fumbled in his pocket for his cellphone. As he was pulling it out, the truck hit a pothole and the phone flew into Elaine's lap.

"Shit. Do me a favour, will you? Find 'Natalie' in the Contacts and call her. Put it on speaker."

She wiped tears from her cheeks and worked his phone in

a few effortless strokes and taps. Tom hadn't realized she was crying. He listened as the call went directly to voicemail.

"This is Natalie Stone. I'm currently out of the country and will return in two weeks. If you'd like to leave a message, do so at the tone. If you want to speak to my EA, press—"

"Kill it," Tom said.

Elaine disconnected.

"Call Jeremy." His teeth rattled as they hit a frost heave and the truck erupted in another symphony of noise. Apparently infrastructure was an issue up here as well as everywhere else in the province.

This time the call was answered: "Dunaway."

"Jeremy, it's Faust. I need—"

"Ah, the great Tom Faust. What brings your delightfully gravelly voice into my headset this morning?"

"I need to talk to my analyst. Who's been assigned to Napier?"

"That would be Trish, but she's at the dentist's office right now having a crown put on."

Tom cursed. Although they'd worked together before, he and Jeremy Dunaway were not a good match. Jeremy resented what he saw as the cowboy attitude of field operatives, particularly those who were ex-cops, and Tom had zero patience for dickheads. He knew Trish to see her, but hadn't worked with her before. Not that it mattered; it was Jeremy or nothing. He was now head of analysis in the Investigations Division, with the appropriate arrogance that went with the promotion. Tom hoped he wouldn't have to browbeat him into helping out.

"You'll have to do this, Jeremy. I need an analysis of satellite surveillance for 17482 Gervais Road, uh, 45.377207 by 78.919374, Algonquin Highlands, Ontario. What's the average range of a drone?"

"A drone? About three kilometers. Say five."

Tom swerved to avoid a pothole and hit another one he hadn't seen. "Jesus Christ. Find me a vehicle parked within a five-kilometer radius of that location or driving up to that location."

"Will do. Are you in a home-made airplane or something? There's a lot of racket in the background."

"Tell me about it. What time is it?"

"It's 9:52 AM."

"Go back as far as seven and forward to now. Get me a face and a plate. Then get me current whereabouts."

"You don't want much, do you?"

"Jeremy, we've got two operatives down and a protectee in imminent danger. I want it all, and I want it now. Get on it, and transfer me to Protective Services."

"Roger that."

Tom was put on hold.

CHAPTER 27

After Tom reported in to Protective Services, explaining that both their operatives were down and presumed to be out, he asked to be transferred to the director, Bryan Weir. While he was waiting, he reached the intersection of County Road 35, where he turned south, passing a Shell station on the left. Reflexively he looked at the gas gauge: still two-thirds of a tank.

Good old Cliff.

His cellphone coughed. "This is Weir speaking."

Tom took the phone from Elaine and tapped it off speaker. "Bryan, it's Tom Faust."

"Hey, Tom. I've just been updated on your situation."

"I'm a hundred and forty klicks north of Lindsay, heading south on 35. I've got the protectee and another person with me right now. Do we have a safe house in Lindsay? I'll also need a babysitter and a vehicle. Preferably a Bronco or a Range Rover."

Napier snorted. "Babysitter."

"We'll have something lined up for you when you get there," Weir said. "Stop at the McDonald's on Kent for coffee. Best in the city."

"Thanks, Bryan." He ended the call and slipped the phone in his pocket.

"I don't get it," Elaine said. "Why do we have to stop for coffee?"

"Spook stuff," Napier said, his camera still trained on Tom.

When they made it to Lindsay, they found the McDonald's on Kent and settled into a booth in the middle of the restaurant. Elaine, being the less-important target, reluctantly agreed to get the coffee. Tom handed her a twenty and told her to get herself a sundae as a reward for being their gofer.

Tom sat facing the side entrance, keeping an eye on everyone who came and went, and he spotted a large mirror in the corner of the ceiling that gave him a view of the aisle behind him. When his coffee was half-finished, two men and a woman entered the restaurant through the side entrance and walked up the aisle. As they passed, one of the men tapped Tom on the shoulder. They sat down at the table behind him.

"Stay put," Tom said, getting up. "I'll just be a minute."

He sat down in the fourth chair at the next table and a short, wiry man held out his hand. "Bill King. I'm your babysitter. Me and Lona Martin." He pointed his thumb at the woman beside him. She shook his hand.

"And that's Spencer beside you," King added. "Give him your keys and he'll get rid of the truck."

Tom dug them out of his pocket and slid them over. Spencer passed a key fob back to him.

"It's the dark green '23 Bronco parked around the side."

"Thanks."

Spencer stood up and offered his hand. "Good luck."

Tom shook his hand. Spencer left the restaurant.

King held out his cellphone. "Call this number for updates. I won't disclose the safe house location right now."

Tom memorized the number.

"Collect their electronics and take them with you. Dispose of them right away."

"The protectee's writing a book. It's on his laptop."

"Mmm." King thought for a moment. "I'll stop somewhere and scrub it for him."

"He's also got a video camera."

"I'll check it over."

"That should be everything," Tom said.

They stood up and move to the next table.

Elaine looked up, ice cream on her upper lip.

"Who's this?" Napier asked.

Tom smiled. "Your new best friend."

CHAPTER 28

Norwood was out jogging, inhaling the city air as though it were a potent drug. It was Wednesday morning, and he was back in Etobicoke, regrouping. He ran west on Dixon Road, maintaining a steady pace, enjoying the exercise.

He nodded at an elderly woman sitting inside a bus shelter as he passed. She looked as though she might have spent the night in there. A few meters later he was at Wincott. He turned right and headed south, apartment towers looming high above him on either side.

He was a townie born and raised, but he loved the city. He loved the smell of traffic and the raging of the big jets overhead, he loved the hustle and bustle of the cars, and he loved the atmosphere of living on the edge, where success or failure could change your life at any moment. Very quietly, or very, very noisily.

He reached Wincott Park and followed the street around the corner, where it became Northcrest Road. Suddenly he was in a neighbourhood of ranch-style houses built close together, cars parked in short driveways, and neatly trimmed shrubs on the front lawns.

He hated them on sight, these shoebox houses. Back home, he had two acres on the edge of town and a three-storey brick Victorian for his kids to grow up in. He didn't mind the condo here in Etobicoke because it was a sanctuary, a base of operations, and its relative smallness didn't bother him. These dumps, however, made him feel suffocated just to look at them. Imagine spending your best years cooped up in one of these wretched places, with a mortgage so high you had to skimp on food so as not to default?

He followed Northcrest to Kipling, where he turned right and headed north back to Dixon. Around the corner, and he was soon jogging into the front lobby of his building.

As he stood in the shower, he ran through yesterday's events once more in his mind. After hearing the pickup truck roar away from the rear of the cottage, he'd used the car that was left running to try to chase them, but he gave up at the first crossroads because he had no idea which way they'd gone. It galled him that Napier had escaped, but there was more to the situation than what Norwood had anticipated in terms of protection, so he decided on a tactical retreat to regroup.

Lathering his chest and arms, he still believed it was the right choice.

He'd driven the car back to the resort. Before leaving, he checked the body of the female protection agent, taking her wallet and identification. He stuffed it into the patch pocket where he'd put the male agent's stuff, then decided it was time to get moving out of there.

He walked up to the ATV trail where he'd left his van. He drove to Huntsville and headed south down Hwy 11 to Orillia, wiping the camouflage paint from his face with a cloth as he went. In Orillia, he parked on a side street in front of an empty lot. Moving into the back of the van, he stripped, shrugged into a change of clothing, stuffed everything except the Mechanixwear gloves into a small haversack, then walked two blocks to a car rental agency. Along the way, he saw a dumpster in the mouth of an alley. He left the haversack there, under a layer of refuse.

He used another false identity to rent a car, which he drove back to the van. He packed all his gear in a rolling suitcase, put the drone in its bag, and transferred everything to the car.

He then took the van to a car wash, drove it through, and had it detailed inside. He parked the van under some trees in the parking lot of a small office building. Using his knife, he punctured a tire and left.

He walked half a block back to the rental car and drove to Toronto, following a circuitous route to shake possible followers. Downtown, he parked in an underground parking lot, where he wiped down the car and walked into the subterranean tunnel system known as PATH.

Extending for some thirty kilometers underground through the downtown, PATH connected pedestrians to more than seventy buildings, three subway stations, hotels, restaurants, and Union Station, not to mention three-and-a-half million square feet of retail space.

What Norwood particularly liked about PATH was the fact that each branch of the network was the responsibility of whoever owned the property through which it ran, totalling over thirty corporations altogether. Each owner contracted their own private security firms for surveillance technology and personnel, and the result was a patchwork quilt in which Norwood had found many gaps and inconsistencies. Whenever he needed to work downtown, PATH was his best friend.

As he moved uptown, he reached the entrance to a clothing

store whose surveillance system was down more than it was up. He bought a new change of clothes and threw the old ones away. He also bought a new knapsack and stuffed the drone into it, after which he ditched the old bag. He destroyed the identification package for that person, along with his cellphone and SIM card.

Knapsack slung over his back and rolling suitcase trailing behind him, he caught the UP train and worked his way north, eventually reaching Dixon Road and home.

As he sat down at the kitchen table for a quick breakfast, he felt reasonably confident that he'd been able to elude any aerial surveillance that might have been trying to track him from Oxtongue Lake. It was an improvement, at least, over his performance at Trent Hills, where he'd blown a fuse and shot Irwin Dessler in the back of the neck with a crossbow.

A *crossbow*, for chrissakes!

He was very disappointed that Napier hadn't shown up in Trent Hills as he'd been expected to. Dessler might still be alive if Norwood had been able to take care of Napier right then and there. An extremely frustrating turn of events. Getting smacked in the mouth while Dessler ran like a spooked deer had morphed his frustration into anger, and the red haze had clouded his judgment.

He had to laugh, though.

A Medieval-style crossbow, for chrissakes. That was a first.

He would dearly have loved to have nailed Napier at the resort, but he had to admit that starting the rental car remotely had been a good trick to draw him away from their escape. He would definitely remember it in the future.

He went into the other room and booted up his laptop. As he waited, he thought about the first time he'd killed someone for money.

He'd kept his gang ties active after getting his carpentry papers, and although his bike-riding days were over, he continue to run errands and do odd jobs for the club president, a guy named Fat Joe McCormick.

McCormick took him under his wing and coached him up in various aspects of the business. Norwood showed basic intelligence, good problem solving, and a steady nerve, and McCormick took a liking to him. He was a heavy drinker, and for a while Norwood tried to keep up with him, but he soon learned he didn't like alcohol, except for an occasional beer, and he didn't like the way it felt to wake up on a cot in one of McCormick's back rooms, hung over and barely human.

A hell of a lot better to let McCormick do his own thing while he sipped a beer and listened to the big man talk. Shit, he loved to talk. War stories; politics; religious philosophy—he was a lapsed Catholic—and anything else that came into his head. What Norwood liked best was when he talked about jobs he'd done in the past, things he'd learned to do and not to do, and how he'd do things better if he had another chance to do them over again.

Eventually the talk worked its way around to the subject of killing. McCormick eased it in gradually, reminiscing about some of the gang executions he'd carried out, witnesses he'd offed, and so on.

He tapped a "1%" patch on his vest and narrowed his eyes at Norwood. "Some AMA asshole claimed one time, way back when, that 99 per cent of bikers were good, law-abiding citizens. That meant we were the 1 percenters, the badassed sons of bitches who made the rest of them look like candy-assed pissants. You get this patch, Craig, when you snuff someone. It means you're a true 1 percenter. Do you understand?"

Norwood understood.

The assignment came not long afterward, in the person of some doofus intruding on their meth business who continued to ignore repeated warnings to get lost. Pretending to set up a drug deal, Norwood met him on a back road where he knifed him, bundled him back into his car, a beat-up Honda, and set the vehicle on fire.

It was an awful mess, and Norwood learned not to burn cars ever again. A rookie mistake. What the hell, he was twenty-four and just getting started.

Norwood rubbed his eyes. His laptop was booted up and ready to go.

Time to get to work.

CHAPTER 29

The first thing Norwood did was to open the video surveillance file from yesterday morning, just before his assault. He paused it when he reached the spot where the two vehicles at the front entrance were visible.

One of them was a black Chevrolet Suburban that likely belonged to the two bodyguards. He opened a drawer and removed the two ID cards on lanyards. Cage Intelligence Group. He zoomed in until the licence plate on the Suburban was visible. He did a frame capture before pulling back to get the plate on the other vehicle. The one that had tricked him into thinking that Napier was trying to escape in it. He captured that frame as well and closed the video file.

Calling up his dark web browser, he navigated to the portal into the various databases he'd hacked. Launching the provincial Department of Motor Vehicles interface, he queried the Suburban's licence plate. As expected, the vehicle was registered to the Cage Intelligence Group. When he ran the other plate, he found it was a rental vehicle. Toggling back to the still, he zoomed in and saw the agency name and city of origin (Peterborough) on the plastic plate holder.

He opened another portal, this time to access the rental agency's Canadian database. A couple of queries found him what he was looking for. The lessee was Thomas T. Faust, Cage Intelligence Group. Didn't bother with a fake identity or anything else, apparently. Another bodyguard? Maybe not. Coming from Peterborough, as opposed to Toronto.

He ran a Google search on the name and found multiple hits detailing the OPP career of Tom Faust, including his adventure with the serial killer known as the Bushmaster in Peterborough County, before and after retirement. There was a trail of promotions, several decorations, and many court appearances as major case manager in serious criminal trials. According to all this stuff, Faust was a regular Wyatt Earp.

There was even an article in a local weekly about Faust having renovated an old decommissioned church in Selwyn as his home. A handyman, to boot. What a hero.

Cops can be dumb, or cops can be very smart. Which was Faust? Would he make the mistake of moving Napier onto his own turf, foolishly hoping for a home-field advantage?

The other thing that bothered Norwood as he digested all this information was the nature of the security surrounding Napier all of a sudden. Cage Intelligence was a shadowy operation. Their website was bare bones: contact information and very little else. Apparently you already had to know who they were and what services they provided before even thinking about talking to them.

So why did little Kenny Napier rate such protection? Was he a secret agent or something? Was the filmmaking stuff a cover for some kind of covert activity that Norwood was in danger of exposing?

At the end of the day, though, Tom Faust was a cop. And

Norwood had never been afraid of cops. Not ever. He knew how to deal with them.

So, his plan now was to start the hunt for Thomas Troy Faust, who would lead him directly to his target, Kenny Napier. Then he could wrap this thing up and catch the next plane to Belize and grab a little beach weather.

CHAPTER 30

The first thing Tom did after leaving the McDonald's on Kent Street was to stop at an electronics store and buy three pre-paid cellphones. He activated one and paired it to the Wi-Fi hands-free setup in the Bronco. He called Jeremy.

He was prepared for the usual bitching and whining, and he wasn't disappointed. Jeremy resented having to do grunt work now that he was a boss, and it annoyed him that there was no one else he could hand it off to at the moment.

Oh, well. Poor boy.

Analysis of the satellite video turned up a white van with licence plates reported stolen from a car in Brampton two years ago. On the video, the van drove up the lane to the entrance of an ATV trail. It pulled over under the cover of a big tree. The assailant launched a drone from the middle of the lane, flew it around for a while, and brought it back. He stowed it in the van and got into the back with it. When he emerged, he went into the forest.

"I'm more interested in what he did after we took off in the truck from the back of the resort."

"After you left, he used your rental car, which was

conveniently left running," his voice heavy with sarcasm, "to attempt pursuit, but he stopped at the first crossroads, apparently realizing that he'd lost you, and he circled back to his van."

"And then?"

"I was able to track the van to Huntsville and south on Highway 11 to Orillia, but we lost him there."

"Shit."

"Yeah, well, Santa Claus still has some presents for you. I'm texting them now."

Tom's phone pinged.

"The first one's a screen grab of your guy as he was flying his drone around. We're running him through our databases but so far, no hits. The second is the best shot of his van that we could get."

"Thanks, Jeremy. Keep it up."

"Yeah. Sure."

Tom opened the file and studied the face. Clean-shaven, forties, strong jaw, closely trimmed dark hair. Sunglasses. Tough-looking. A professional.

He opened the other file. The van was white and unmarked. The licence plate was not visible.

Tom threw the Bronco into gear and headed out of town.

Someone hired this guy to take out Kenneth Napier. Why? Why? Something connected to his autobiography, apparently, but what?

Tom had been a detective for most of his life. He'd tracked and captured subjects on less information than this.

Once a cop, always a cop. Time to begin the hunt.

CHAPTER 31

When Tom reached Beaverton, a village of just under three thousand souls, he stopped at a small computer store and went inside.

The young man behind the counter glanced up, saw that it was some elderly looking stranger and not one of his friends, and slowly put down the miniature screwdriver he was using to disassemble some unrecognizable piece of hardware. He flipped up his magnifying glasses and smiled.

"Help you?"

Tom put his phone down on the counter. "I've got a couple of jaypegs I'd like to get printed out. Is that something you could do for me?"

The kid rubbed his neckbeard cautiously. "Suppose. They're not porn, are they?"

Tom laughed. "No, they're not porn." He took out his licence and flashed it. "Private investigator."

The kid looked at the ID, looked at Tom, and grinned. "Wow. No kidding. A real PI. Right here in beautiful li'l B-town."

"Can you print them out for me?"

"Sure. Piece of cake. How many copies?"

"Give me five of each."

"Sure. Show me which ones."

Tom navigated to the shot of the assailant. The kid took the phone and texted it to himself. "What's the other one?"

"The white vehicle."

"Oh yeah. I see it." He sent it to himself as well, then handed Tom's phone back. "It'll take just a minute. I'm switching to our best printer."

He used his own phone to start the print job. "So, are you from around here?"

Because he was feeling good about being able to get hard copies of the photos here in the middle of Bumcrack, Ontario, Tom was in a tolerant mood.

"No, passing through. On my way to Orillia."

"Story of this town's life, I guess. I was born and raised here. My mom's the school principal."

"Is that right." Tom listened to the sound of a printer starting up in the next room.

"It's not a bad place. Bet you didn't know that movies have been shot here."

Tom suddenly felt like this case was snowing him under in an avalanche of cinematography. Or whatever the hell you'd call it. You couldn't swing a dead cat around without hitting somebody or something connected to the movies.

"Which ones?"

The kid grinned. "Well, for one thing, did you know the cult classic *Cannibal Girls* was filmed right here in town?"

"I did not know that."

"Yeah. It was directed by the guy who did *Ghostbusters* and *Meatballs*. Ivan Reitman. And the star was the *Schitt's Creek* guy. You know. Eugene Levy. Of course, this was back in the early 70s. Before I was born. Still. Plus the movies *Jasper, Texas* with Jon Voigt, and *Dead of Winter*, which was directed by Arthur Penn. The guy who did *Bonnie and Clyde* and *The Miracle Worker* with Patty Duke. Sorry, I'm a bit of a film geek, but I gotta tell you, we're like Hollywood North up here."

"I thought that was supposed to be the Muskokas."

"Nah. They just get vacationing celebrities. We get the movie makers. Or we did, anyway. Before I was born."

He went into the back room and came back with a group of printouts. Handing them to Tom, he said, "The other one's just printing now. So, who's the guy?"

"Some guy."

"You chasing him?"

"You could say that. Seen him before?"

"No, thank God. He looks like a mean prick. What do you want him for?"

"Killed a couple of my co-workers."

"Jesus! That's incredible!"

They heard the printer stop printing.

"Excuse me." The kid went back to retrieve the prints of the van. "So is this his vee-hicle?"

Tom nodded. "What do I owe you?"

"Ten prints? Ten bucks."

Tom paid in cash.

"Do you want me to delete them from my phone? I could keep them in case the guy comes through and I see him. I could let you know."

Tom dug out a business card and gave it to him.

"Sounds like an idea. Just don't approach him or engage him in any way. He's a deadly killer."

"Wow," the kid said, putting Tom's card in his pocket.

CHAPTER 32

The drive to Orillia took Tom about another half hour. On the way, he decided to try to find the van first and the man second, figuring that his odds were better with the former than with the latter. When he reached town, he drove to the street where the satellite had lost track of the vehicle, working on the theory that the assailant abandoned it and switched to another set of wheels. He cruised up and down the streets, looking in parking lots and along the curbs. No white van. It was more than possible, he decided, that it had been towed away this morning from wherever it had been parked overnight.

He turned at the next intersection and began to work his way to the south end of the city. He was willing to bet that Reliable Towing and Storage still had the contract with the OPP, who handled both city and rural policing services, and with the city bylaw officers, who wrote out the parking tickets.

He drove to their yard and walked inside the office. A man dragged himself from behind a desk and came up to the counter. He was in his fifties with a grey comb-over, unshaven jowls, and small dark eyes. He wore a short-sleeved company shirt with an embroidered patch above the pocket that said "Don."

Tom had never seen him before. He snapped his PI card down on the counter and asked if they'd taken in a white van this morning. Don reached out an index finger, pulled the card close, looked at it, and pushed it back to Tom.

"I'm not allowed to give out that information."

For the thousandth time, Tom missed his badge and warrant card. He took out his wallet and pulled a twenty partway out. Don snorted. Tom pushed it back in and pulled out a fifty.

"Came in just before ten thirty."

"Can I see it?"

"Sorry, unauthorized access to the impound area is not allowed."

Tom tufted out the twenty again. "And I want to look at the paperwork."

Don tapped the counter.

Tom put the two bills down. They quickly disappeared.

Don brought him a file from a battered metal filing cabinet covered with stickers, magnetic give-aways, and keys on rings. According to the photocopy of the guy's driver's licence, he was using the alias "Ian MacDonald." His date of birth was May 17, 1977, and his address was 18 Newdawn Crescent, Scarborough, Ontario. A Visa card and the vehicle registration confirmed the details.

Tom photographed everything with his phone and put it back into the file. Don put the file back in the cabinet and lifted the gate for Tom to follow him back into the employee area and out into the yard.

The vehicle was a 2018 GMC Savannah cargo van, white. Tom put on a pair of latex gloves. "Were you inside the vehicle?"

"Didn't need to be. Jim offloaded it right where you see it."

"Jim Who?"

"McDaniels. Cousin of mine. Good guy. Real honest."

"No one else touches this until the police arrive.

Understood?"

"Sure. What the hell. I've got better things to do. You done here?"

"I'll meet you back in the office."

Don took the hint and shuffled off.

Tom gave the van a good going-over without getting inside. He found the VIN plate and wrote the number down in his notebook. He noticed the punctured tire, obviously made with a knife. Opening the various doors and eyeballing the interior, he saw nothing useful. It was empty. Sanitized, no doubt. On the passenger side, he dropped open the glove compartment. Empty.

Definitely a pro.

CHAPTER 33

Tom walked into Hospitality Rent-A-Car, where a middle-aged woman was vacuuming the carpet in the front customer area. Hearing the door open behind her, she turned around, snapping off the vacuum cleaner.

"Tommy Faust, in the living flesh! How the hell are you, darling?"

"Hello, Mary. I'm well. You?"

"Fine. Gerald passed away a year ago, but I'm slowly getting over it."

Tom grimaced. "I'm very sorry to hear that. My condolences."

Mary Prentice had been with the rental agency for over 20 years. She always liked to flirt with Tom. He'd never met her husband, John Prentice, who had owned the franchise. Now, evidently, it was hers.

"Where did you retire to, Tommy?"

"Peterborough County. Bought an old church and renovated it."

"A church! Getting religion on us?"

Laughing, he showed her his PI card.

"You're private now. Good for you. I always thought you'd be one of the ones who'd need to stay busy."

He handed her a copy of the assailant's photograph. "Did this guy come in yesterday?"

She stared at it for a moment. "Yeah, he did. Quiet fellow. All business and no small talk. No GPS, no frills."

She walked around behind the counter and pounded on a keyboard. Then she clicked with the mouse and turned the monitor so he could see it.

"Daniel Garnet Freeman," she read out loud. "D-O-B 1979-9-22. Address 1248 Maplewood Drive, Brampton, Ontario. Driver's licence, Visa."

Tom wrote the information down in his notebook, not wanting to photograph her screen with its proprietary information showing. If Kate Greene wanted to get a warrant for it, that would be up to her.

Mary brought up the scan of Daniel Freeman's driver's licence. It was the same man as the one on Ian MacDonald's licence: clean-shaven; a firm jaw, creased forehead; cold blue eyes. Dark hair trimmed very short, military-fashion. Height listed as 188 cm which, converted into Imperial measurement, was six feet and one-and-a-half inches. The guy looked solid.

The vehicle Freeman had rented was a 2024 Toyota RAV4, silver with black trim. Tom jotted down the licence plate number.

"Thanks."

Mary swung the monitor back around. "Am I going to get beat on this one?"

"I don't know." Tom put away his notebook. "I'll do my best to get it back to you in one piece, but—"

"No guarantees," she finished. "I know. I appreciate the

sentiment, though."

She came back around the counter and stood at the window, watching the traffic in the street.

"I'm thinking of retiring too," she said over her shoulder. "Sell the franchise and go someplace warm. At one point it would have been Florida, but with what's going on down there now, I wouldn't go within a thousand miles of that zoo."

"How about the south of France?" Tom suggested. "You're bilingual."

She turned and, smiling, gave him a long hug. "Take care of yourself, Tom. Cop business is always dangerous business, private or public."

"I will. You too."

She kissed him on the cheek and pushed him in the direction of the door.

CHAPTER 34

Tom spotted Kate Greene in a back booth of the local burger joint on Memorial Avenue. She gave him a quick wave, and he slid onto the bench seat across the table from her.

A server appeared immediately, and Tom ordered coffee.

"The food's just as bad as always," Kate said, a hand around her own cup. "This isn't much better."

She'd picked it as a place to meet because it was unpopular with most of the staff working at General Headquarters, and they wouldn't be noticed. As with many other major case managers, she lived in Orillia and travelled to crime scenes within her area of jurisdiction. She was staying in a hotel down in Cobourg while the Dessler investigation was ongoing, but had come up to GHQ to attend a meeting. She didn't say what the meeting was about, and Tom didn't particularly care.

"I'm passing this information to you right now," Tom began, putting a file folder down on the table, "because I'm not sure how long it will take for Cage to process and forward it, given that Natalie Stone is currently out of the country." He'd sent everything to Jeremy Dunaway for analysis, but he wasn't sure what would happen to it after that.

"Plus," Kate said over the rim of her cup, "you don't want to be obstructing an official investigation by withholding information."

"There's that, too." Taking out his phone, he promptly began to withhold information. He described the assault that had taken place at the resort on Oxtongue Lake, where Napier had been sheltering in place. He withheld the fact that two of Cage's people had been slaughtered by the assailant. Cage Intelligence's janitorial services had cleaned it up, removing all trace of Bradley and Cohen, and had only reported the murder of Cliff Bruckner to the OPP. So it was in connection with Cliff's homicide that Tom was providing to Kate his information.

"Given the use of a garrotte, and the organized nature of the attack, like using a drone for surveillance and other things, I'd hazard a guess we're dealing with a professional assassin."

He gave her a copy of the printout, and tapped on his phone. "I'll send you the electronic version."

"Thanks. Did you make an ID?"

Tom snorted. "Two, so far." He opened the file. "Ian MacDonald." He passed her a printout of the licence the assailant had used while driving the white van.

"Daniel Garnett Freeman. Current lessee of this vehicle," he recited the information on the car the man had rented from Mary Prentice.

"He ditched his old ride, the van, here in the city." He gave her a copy of the satellite photo. "A 2018 GMC Savannah, no plates, VIN" –he read it off—"currently in the impound lot of Reliable Towing and Storage. It's possible the tire tread marks will match something from the Dessler crime scene. We're dealing with a professional killer, not an amateur, so there are no guarantees. Plus, he may have missed something when he sanitized it. You never know; you may get lucky."

"So you're telling me you think there's a direct connection between the Dessler killing and Kenneth Napier."

"That's what I'm telling you, Kate. But as an anonymous tip. You'll have to build your own case."

"Where's Napier right now? He needs to come in and we'll give him protective custody. Is he here?"

"Kate, Kate. Nice try. He's much safer where he is right now."

He stood up, dropping a ten on the table to cover the coffees and tip. "I'll be in touch."

He felt her eyes on his back as he left the restaurant.

CHAPTER 35

On Thursday morning, Norwood rode the GO Train to Oshawa. It was an hour trip, and he spent the time thinking about his kids.

Sophia, the youngest, was her mother's little angel. She had sandy hair like her mom, blue eyes, and a plumpness that reminded everyone of a little cherub. She also had her mother's sweet disposition, and the rocking horse Norwood was making for her was without doubt a labour of love.

Jennifer, the middle girl, was six. She reminded Norwood of *his* mother—quiet; a bit of a loner; not too smart. Sharon had had her tested and there was no indication of a learning disability that had a label attached to it, but the truth was that she was a bit slow. In Grade One, she was still a little behind the rest of the kids in writing skills and arithmetic. Like Norwood's mother, she was easy to get along with and long-suffering with others. Sometimes, though, Norwood thought she went out of her way to get involved in the troubles of other people.

Elizabeth, eight, was the oldest. Everyone called her Betty. Her personality, unfortunately, tended more toward Norwood's than her mother's—quieter than Jen and another loner. But she did well in school and liked to spend her spare time reading. Norwood wasn't sure what would become of Betty. He expected that her adolescence would be hard and she'd end up diagnosed with chronic depression, anxiety disorder, and all the rest of it.

Norwood worried about the girls, even little Sophia, but he was very glad they weren't boys. He was convinced a boy would have had no choice but to grow up like his father, even though Sharon was a much better mother than his own had been. The last thing he wanted was a child following in his footsteps.

He got off at the Oshawa transit station on Bloor Street and took a taxi downtown. He walked six blocks to a ramshackle four-storey apartment building. Around the back was a small parking lot for tenants and ground-level indoor parking to accommodate four more vehicles. The door was opened by inserting a key into a lock cemented into a pillar at car-window height. Norwood inserted a key, watched the door slowly roll up, and went inside.

The four cars inside were all expensive models. Three were covered with dust and the fourth had a tarpaulin thrown over it. He pulled off the tarp, wadded it up, and tossed it in the corner. The car was a 2020 E 450 4MATIC Mercedes-Benz mid-size sedan. Norwood was glad to see it was undisturbed from the last time he'd visited, a couple of years ago. It wasn't the best neighbourhood in the city, but he'd nosed around and learned that the building had had relatively few break-ins.

The Mercedes was a bit of an extravagance. He'd wanted a backup vehicle stashed east of Toronto that he could get to in a pinch, and he'd splurged fifty grand on this one because he was coming off a very successful job in California and felt like rewarding himself. It was a really nice car, with a lot of bells and whistles. It had had no winter driving so far in its mechanical life, so everything still worked to spec. He started it up and let it rev for a few minutes to clear its throat of accumulated dust and carbon.

He drove to the nearest 401 on-ramp and headed east, all the way down to Port Hope, where he exited and took Highway 28 north toward Peterborough. Bypassing the city, he continued north, navigating to Bridgenorth, and from there made his way to Cedar Hill Road. He drove down Cedar Hill a bit and turned into the driveway of Tom Faust's church, parking behind a Lincoln Town Car that he understood was Faust's personally owned vehicle.

He put on a pair of latex gloves and did a quick tour around the church, admiring the solid stonework, the Norman-style tower at the front, and the neatly kept landscaping around the place. He had to hand it to Faust: it was a very nice little property.

Checking the windows, he saw no sign of activity inside. So Theory One, that Faust would be dumb enough to take Napier home with him, was out.

The front door was secured with a deadbolt lock, but Norwood knew from experience that if a lock opened with a key, it could be picked. This one was a good brand, and it took a little longer than he would have wished, but Norwood was soon inside and disarming the security system.

He strolled around, the carpenter in him admiring the wooden beams, wainscoting, and pine board floors. Nice, nice, nice. He wondered how much of the work Faust had done himself and how much he'd contracted out.

He gave it a cursory search. There was no landline telephone, so no answering machine to listen to for messages containing hints Norwood could follow up on. He riffled through the paper on Faust's desk and found nothing other than bills, flyers, and other such junk.

In the middle of the nave, he paused for a moment and looked up at the rafters. He could plainly see the mark the rope had made when the guy had been strung up to get Faust's attention in the Bushmaster case he'd read about online. He briefly considered leaving a calling card of his own, but quickly dismissed the idea. McCormick had taught him never to sign his own work, advice that related not only to his methods of execution but also his presence anywhere. Anonymity was his friend. In and out. On to the next one.

He took a few photographs. He looked at the personal photos on end tables in the living room area. He recognized Faust's daughter, the famous actress. He looked at the framed portrait of a woman that was signed: "To Tom with all my love, Kelly."

Ex-wife? Girlfriend?

He photographed them all and then let himself out.

CHAPTER 36

After leaving Orillia, Tom drove down to Brampton to check out the address on Daniel Freeman's driver's licence. Maplewood Drive turned out to be a very nice street in an upper-middle-class neighbourhood. Number 1248 was a smart-looking bungalow with a two-car garage and an attractive rock garden in the middle of the front lawn. Tom parked in the driveway and knocked on the door.

A white-haired woman in a Chinese-style housecoat opened the door. "Yes?"

Tom held up his licence. "My name's Tom Faust. I'm looking for Daniel Freeman. Is he here?"

"Oh, dear." Her hand flew to her cheek. "Are you the police?"

"No, ma'am, I'm a private investigator. May I come in for a moment?"

"Private investigator. My. Yes." She stepped back. "Please come in."

It was a beautiful home, carefully furnished and immaculately maintained. She led him into a sitting room. He declined an offer of coffee or tea, and got back to the point.

"Daniel Freeman, ma'am? Is he here?"

"I'm sorry, I've never heard that name before in my life."

"May I ask your name?"

"Carson. Patricia Carson. My husband's John. He's not here right now. He took the car to Canadian Tire for a new set of summer tires."

"I see. What kind of car is it?"

"A Jaguar. I'm not sure what year."

"Is it possible one of your relatives, maybe a son or daughter or grandchild, would know Daniel Freeman?"

"We have no children. Just John and I."

"Maybe Freeman lived here before you?"

"We bought it new in 1981, so, no."

"Maybe the realtor?"

"She was a woman. Renata Quill. A name that's hard to forget, don't you think?"

"What time will your husband be back?"

"He only left a few minutes before you knocked, so, it'll probably be a couple of hours. They're not exactly Speedy Gonzaleses at that place."

Tom gave her a card and asked her to get her husband to call if the name Daniel Freeman meant anything to him. Out in the car, he plugged Ian MacDonald's Scarborough address into the GPS and pulled out of the driveway, thinking that he was wasting his time. False identities almost never provided a thread worth following up on, but they needed to be looked into no matter what. It was part of the job.

Newdawn Crescent was crammed into a tiny rectangle of very expensive land sided by Finch Avenue and Brimley Road in Scarborough. The home at Ian MacDonald's address was a storey-and-a-half townhouse with a garage, a stubby driveway, and a patchy lawn shared with the residents next door. Tom parked at the curb and knocked at the front door.

A woman of East Indian descent opened the door. "Yes?"

Tom held up his licence. "My name's Tom Faust. I'm looking for Ian MacDonald. Is he here?"

"I'm sorry, you have the wrong place. No one by that name lives here."

"May I ask your name?"

"Who did you say you are?"

Tom held out his licence. She took it, studied the photo and compared it to him. "I'm not sure why a private investigator is coming to my door. Dhruv!"

A man appeared behind her, looking at Tom over her shoulder. She gave him Tom's licence. "What do you think?"

He studied the photo on the licence, compared it to Tom's face with its carefully neutral expression, and gave it back to her. "I don't know what a private investigator would want with us."

"Just a couple of questions. May I come in for a moment?"

"No," Dhruv said. "Please ask your questions where you are."

"Okay. Does the name Ian MacDonald mean anything to you?"

"Nothing."

Tom looked at the woman. "Ma'am?"

"No. Who is he?"

"Is it possible this MacDonald is connected to you or your family in some way? Or maybe a co-worker or a previous tenant at this address?"

"I don't know this person. Dhruv?"

"No. I'm self-employed in high tech, so there are no co-workers."

"Someone who previously lived here?"

"I have no idea. Aren't there websites where a private investigator can look up such things?"

"Yeah, there are." Tom gave the woman a card. "If you think of someone or something connected to Ian MacDonald, I'd appreciate a call."

The woman looked at the card and passed it over her shoulder to Dhruv, who glanced at it and put it into his shirt pocket.

Back in the car, Tom decided to make one more stop before calling it a day. He wanted to have another word with Judd Hendrick, run these names by him, see if anything rang a bell. He threw Hendrick's office address into the GPS and headed off.

When he finally reached the Apple Creek business park in Markham, he was starting to feel tired. He decided that after seeing Hendrick, he'd find a motel room and hole up for the night.

The receptionist at the front desk shook her head when he asked to see Judd Hendrick. "I'm sorry, sir, Mister Hendrick is not available."

"Did he go home already?"

"I'm sorry, sir. I'm not at liberty to say."

"Maybe I could see Vanessa Black, then."

"I'm very sorry, sir. She's not available, either."

"What the hell?"

The woman frowned at him. "You were here last Friday, weren't you?"

"That's right. I saw both of them."

The woman hesitated. "May I see your identification again,

please?"

Tom brought out his licence.

"Mister Hendrick is missing, Mister Faust. He hasn't been seen since last Sunday."

Tom wasn't able to hide his surprise. "Missing? Did he take a sudden vacation or something?"

"The police have been looking into it. They've talked to me twice, but I don't know what happened. Ms. Black filed a missing person's report on Tuesday. There's been no word at all."

Tom was about to express his annoyance, but instead he thanked the woman and walked out, jaw clenched. In the car, he added it up. Judd Kendrick knew the whereabouts of Ken Napier. The assailant showed up at that exact location to make an attempt on Napier's life. Kendrick has disappeared. The assailant must have extracted Napier's location from Kendrick while removing him from the picture. Most likely on a permanent basis.

Should he follow up on Kendrick's disappearance? To see if the assailant had made any mistakes or left a thread of some kind behind?

The reality of the situation was that he was just too tired to do any more today. As much as he hated to admit it, his energy level was a bit lower than it had been when he was forty.

It would be much more prudent to call Kate Greene, make sure she was better informed about Kendrick's disappearance than he'd been, and call it a day.

He googled motels in Richmond Hill and started shopping for a room.

CHAPTER 37

The following morning, Tom woke up from a convoluted dream about walking a beat in an unknown city to find himself in a strange room. It took him a moment to remember where he was and why he'd gone to roost here last night.

The buzzing sound that had disturbed him was coming from his cellphone, sitting on the night table next to his ear. Propping himself up on one elbow, he put on his glasses and looked at the call display: CIG.

"Faust."

"Good morning, Mister Faust. I hope I haven't disturbed you."

He glanced at the time in the corner of the screen: 7:42 AM. More or less his usual time to get up in the morning.

"No. Who is this?"

"Trish Hatt, at your service, sir."

The woman had a wicked Cockney accent and an obnoxiously cheery attitude. "Hatt? You're with Cage, are you?"

"I've woken you up, haven't I? I'm very sorry, sir. Mister Dunaway wanted me to call you right away."

Dunaway. Trish. "You're Trish."

"Yes, sir."

"How are you feeling, Trish? You were ill yesterday, weren't you?"

"I was at the dentist's, having a crown put on. But here I am, good as new."

Tom dragged himself out of bed and crossed the room to the bathroom. "Wait one, will you?"

"Yes, sir."

He put her on hold and relieved himself. He splashed cold water on his face and felt more awake. He sat down on the chair in front of the little desk, took the phone off hold, and put her on speaker.

"Still there?"

"Still here. I've done an analysis of the information you sent in yesterday, and I thought you'd best have a quick rundown on it before you hit the road this morning."

"All right. Fire away."

"I'm not sure how much you know about this kind of fraud, Mister Faust."

"Just Tom. Please. False identities? Not very much. They came up a few times in cases I managed, but my level of expertise is right around the same level as a bartender or a club bouncer."

Trish giggled, a startling sound. "Well, it's your lucky day, Tom, because it happens to be my particular area of expertise. Isn't that just brilliant?"

"It is. So, what have you got."

"I—"

Suddenly, the penny dropped. Hatt. Cage. His de facto boss on this case, Brenda Cage, had been Brenda Hatt before she married the head honcho. "You're related to Mrs. Cage."

"Oh dear, you've found me out. Guilty as charged. She's my Auntie Brenda. My da's her big brother."

"I see. And Sean Cage is your uncle."

"A true detective. There you go. Although, before you go thinking I'm an outrageous case of nepotism with absolutely no competence, let me take a moment to introduce myself."

Tom said nothing.

"I'll take that as an affirmative. I have three university degrees: one in math; one in information technology; and one in public administration. That last one, I have to admit, was sheer curiosity.

"At any rate, my real education came on Uncle Sean's knee. Almost everything I know about intelligence I learned by the time I was twelve. I pestered him without mercy at family gatherings. It got so he had to take me for a little walk down the street so others wouldn't hear what we were saying. I was such a pest."

"Okay."

"Yes, quite enough. Down to business. First of all, what we're talking about here are *synthetic* identities. That's the *mot du jour* in the industry when you're looking at fake identity. Now, there are several different kinds of synthetic IDs, and they're mostly used in financial fraud, but sometimes they're for stuff like what your guy's into. Travel, movement and accommodations, car rentals, stuff like that."

"Yes."

"The two you sent in are what we folks in the business like to call *Frankenstein* identities. These guys take real, legitimate PII chunks—personally identifiable information—from a bunch of different sources and mash them together into an identity that's completely unreal. Frankenstein. Like, who was *he* when he was alive? Now he's just a bunch of body parts sewn together. Give you the screaming abdabs, as my mum likes to say.

"Anyways, they're tough to pick up on, because any given PII chunk will connect to a real identity somewhere in a system verification, instead of raising a red flag as a fake chunk of information that bounces as a null result. Get what I mean?"

"Yes."

"So real addresses but the wrong people. Real SINs but young kids who are deceased, which are great because then it becomes a fun fill-in-the-blank game with other random PII. One more thing. These two particular sets of ID have a signature—I mean, they fit a profile I'm familiar with."

Tom had only been half-listening, but his ears suddenly perked up. "Tell me more."

"Sure. Does the name Frank Harvey mean anything to you?"

Tom thought for a moment. It rang a bell. Five or six years ago, wasn't it? A couple of years after he retired and settled down in Selwyn. He remembered talking to Gavin Elliott about the guy. Remembered how pleased Gavin was that they'd finally caught up with him. Gavin was director of the Criminal Investigation Branch by then, and a superintendent.

"Con artist, wasn't he?"

"An artist, for sure, but of the ID forgery kind. The OPP, your old friends, arrested a guy with a messenger bag full of synthetic ID documents and he grassed on poor old Frank. They set up a sting and nailed him in Newmarket."

"Long story short?" Tom prompted.

"This is his work. His stuff was excellent, first rate, but he tended to go back to the same sources for his PII bits. Later in his career, especially. It becomes a signature for those of us who can read this particular sort of tea leaves."

"You're sure of this? MacDonald-slash-Freeman didn't do it himself?"

"Noo, no, this is high-level pro stuff, as I said. Frank Harvey stuff."

"I'd like to talk to this Harvey guy," Tom said, more to himself than to the phone.

"Well, you'd better hurry."

"Why's that?"

"He's in palliative care in a hospice in Vaughan, that's why. About to breathe his last breath at any moment."

"He got parole?"

"Compassionate. Cancer."

Tom thought quickly. Vaughan was only about a half an hour west of where he was. Time for a shower and shave, fresh change of clothes, and breakfast before looking up the guy who'd provided the assailant with his false—synthetic—IDs. "Could you send me the address of this place?"

"That's what I love about you Canadians." She laughed. "You don't throw out orders, you ask politely."

Tom's phone pinged.

"That's it there," she said. "Let me know if you need anything else."

"I will. Thanks."

She was already gone.

CHAPTER 38

Tom pulled into the parking lot at the front of the Marco and Pietro Ferraro Hospice on Rutherford Road in Vaughan and admired the surroundings as he slowly walked toward the main entrance.

A modern-looking, two-storey building with two ground-floor wings, one at ten o'clock and the other at two o'clock, it had been built in a green oasis on the western edge of the city. With only sixteen beds and privately owned, it was a difficult place to get into, but Frank Harvey had apparently been taken care of as soon as his parole was granted and he needed a place to receive palliative care.

Manila envelope in hand, he told the receptionist he was looking for Nurse Dorothy Connors, that they'd spoken on the phone and she was expecting him. He was given directions to the nursing station at the intersection of the two wings.

The place was quiet, except for music playing through the public address system. It was probably part of their therapy program, where the music was intended to reduce stress and improve the mood of residents. It was some kind of instrumental stuff, slow and comforting, and the volume was turned down to little more than a whisper.

Tom figured if he dropped into one of the big armchairs in the front foyer, he'd be asleep inside of five minutes.

Nurse Connors was tall, middle-aged, and Black. She nodded when he introduced himself and led him to a door directly across from the nurse's station that opened into the outdoor space between the wings.

"You'll find Mister Harvey in the alcove," she said, holding the door open for him.

"Thanks."

He started down a path in the middle of what was an extensive and very beautiful garden. On either side, banks of spring flowers blossomed: red, yellow, and purple tulips; daffodils; and other plants Tom thought might be bleeding heart. He passed lilac bushes and cherry blossom trees adding to the attractiveness of the place. Tom considered himself a poor hand as a gardener, but he liked being around spaces that were obviously well tended by people who knew what they were doing.

There were windows on either side, probably to give residents a view of the garden from their room. Toward the back, at the end of the path, was the aforementioned alcove, a sturdy-looking little brick structure with an arched entrance, windows in the back, and a tile floor. Tom could see two men inside, sitting on a white iron bench.

He passed a wheelchair that had been parked to the side and stopped a few meters short of the arch. "I'm Tom Faust. I'm here to see Mister Harvey."

One of the men, white haired and dressed in black, stood up and offered his hand. "I'm Father Joe Marcuzzi. This is Frank."

The other man leaned forward and held out his hand. He

was small and shrunken, his bald head covered in liver spots, his face gaunt and his eyes sunken. Tom took his hand carefully, felt a gentle squeeze, and let go.

"I'm Harvey." His voice rattled in his throat. "You a cop, Mister Faust?"

Father Joe indicated a chair that had been brought out for Tom's use. "Please. Sit down."

Tom sat. "Used to be. Pulled the pin and went private."

"OPP, I bet. The guys who got me."

"Yeah." He showed him his licence. "Private, now."

"Time to make some real money, eh?"

"Yeah. So, you feel up to talking for a few minutes?" He glanced at the priest, who nodded.

"Oh, yeah. Sure, sure. And don't mind the padre, here. We go back a ways. Brother-in-law. My wife's a Marcuzzi. Plus, he's nice to me even though I ain't Catholic."

"It's never too late," Father Joe murmured.

Harvey laughed, coughed, subsided.

Tom gave him a moment before starting in.

"I have a couple of packages we believe were yours. May I show them to you?"

"Mine? Let's see them."

Tom put the envelope on his lap and drew out the contents. MacDonald was on top, so he started there. Father Joe held out his hand, and Tom gave him the printouts one at a time: driver's licence; provincial health card; Visa; bank convenience card.

Harvey studied each one as Father Joe held them out to him, but said nothing. Father Joe gave them back, and Tom tucked them under the envelope. He passed over the Freeman printouts, and the same routine followed.

Tom stuffed everything back into the envelope. "So?"

"Cancer started in the liver," Harvey said, "and spread everywhere else. They figure I got about a month left. Damn shame. But for some reason my brain was spared. I can still think good, and I can still remember. That's my work, Mister Faust. Most definitely. Both packages."

"Who'd you sell them to?"

"That's what you came here to find out, ain't it?"

"Yes, sir. It is."

"Well, let's see." Harvey closed his eyes and let his head fall back. "I was in the business nearly forty years before you boys caught up with me. Started forging cheques when I was a kid. Schoolboy tricks."

He motioned with his hand. "Padre, do you mind? A nip of the good stuff?"

Father Joe picked up a water bottle, held it to Harvey's mouth, and gave it a squeeze. Harvey swallowed, coughed, swallowed.

Tom caught the aroma of alcohol. Vodka, he guessed. Or maybe aqua vitae, blessed by the priest and valued over the centuries for its medicinal qualities. Ethanol with a punch.

"Where was I?" he wheezed as Father Joe dabbed at the corner of his mouth with a handkerchief.

"Hanging bad paper," Tom said.

"Yeah. Right." He coughed again, and grinned at Tom. "Believe it or not, that actually cuts the nausea. For a few minutes, anyways."

Tom looked at Father Joe, who winked.

"I apprenticed with one of the best in the game," Harvey continued. "He's dead now, so I guess it's okay if I say his name. Angel Falcone. Little guy. Sorta like me, I guess. Quiet as a mouse. But the hands and eyes of an angel, believe me."

Tom hadn't anticipated serving as an audience for Harvey's life story, having come here, as the ex-con had recognized, just to get a name. But he understood what was happening. The man was near death. Harvey could hear the door opening, and he was about to walk through. Before he did, though, he wanted one more chance to tell someone who he'd been while he was still alive and walking above the ground.

"Good man, Mister Falcone. Taught me right. Passed along a lot of his customers when he retired."

"When was this?" Tom asked, to show an interest.

"Ooh, jeez, let me see. I'm what, sixty now?" He glanced at Father Joe. "When did Mister Falcone pass on?"

"Ninety-five, I think." The priest pinched his nose, trying to remember.

"Sounds about right. Anyways, I learned from the best. And it's a good thing, cuz when the synthetic ID fraud game exploded, I was busier than a one-armed paperhanger. If you know what I mean."

"Uh huh."

"Guys were coming to me for bundles, not just one or two. Just before the pandemic hit, I was handling orders of up to four hundred IDs, all different, all for the same guys. Imagine that, now."

He looked at Father Joe, raised his eyebrow, and received another shot of the water of life.

After coughing and clearing his throat, he turned a sheepish eye on Tom. "I shoulda known that cop was stinging me, cuz he only ordered ten. Way lower than most other customers at that point in time."

Tom tapped the envelope in his lap. "And how about this guy?"

"He wanted an even hundred. Tough kid, but I kinda liked him. No bullshit. Pardon me, Father. Said he needed to burn through some of them and use others for a longer period of time. I got the feeling he was in a different business than most of the other guys, if you know what I mean."

"I know exactly what you mean. So you met him? In person?"

Harvey nodded. "He sent me a couple of passport photos, but they were crap. I wouldn't use them on a library card. He suggested we meet. I said okay, but I was a little worried I wouldn't live through the occasion, so when he showed up I was wearing a kevlar vest and a helmet. He laughed like crazy, so I figured I was okay."

"Tell me you got his real name."

"Not at the time. He never mentioned it. Paid in cash. A nice bundle, believe you me. But after, I reached out to a couple of contacts. One of them happened to know the guy from when he was a biker kid. Norwood, he was called. Craig Norwood. I'm pretty sure that was his real handle."

CHAPTER 39

When Tom knocked on the door of the small frame house on a quiet street in north Lindsay, it was opened by an elderly man wearing a track suit and carpet slippers.

"Are you Mister Palmer?" Tom asked.

"Yes, I am. May I help you?" He was tall and lean, his hair was white, and his manner was polite and pleasant.

"I'm here to see Mister Green."

"Please come inside."

Tom stepped into the hallway as Mr. Palmer closed the door behind him. He waited while the man whispered away into a side room. After a moment, Bill King came out and shook his hand.

"You weren't followed?"

Tom shook his head. "How's it going here?"

"Quiet. He's waiting for you."

Tom followed him down the hall and into the kitchen. Mr. Palmer, the owner and resident of the house, was nowhere in sight. Lona Martin was leaning against the counter, arms folded. She nodded at Tom, her expression betraying exasperation. Elaine sat in a chair in the corner, quiet as a mouse.

Napier was sitting on a high stool in front of his video camera, which he'd manage to set up on a tripod despite the fact that he hadn't had one with him when they'd taken off from the resort. Perhaps Mr. Palmer was a photography bug and had loaned it to him.

Napier waved. "The wanderer returns. Have you found my tormenter yet and taken care of him?"

"Getting close," Tom said. "What's with the setup?"

"Catching up on my interviews. Lona and Bill co-operated, although Mister Palmer politely turned me down, and no one would let me shoot the other rooms or the exterior." He grinned. "Now it's my turn to be interviewed. That's why you're here, right?"

"That's right." Tom stood behind the kitchen chair that had been set up beside the camera. "I don't like all this, though. You shouldn't be taping. I'm sure Bill and Lona have explained the risks to you."

Lona nodded imperceptibly.

"Of course they did; they're pros. That's why I feel safe. You guys aren't going to let this lunatic get within a hundred klicks of me, are you?"

"We've already had one close call," Tom said, sitting down. "We don't want another one."

"Understood. But explain to me what you've found out."

Tom glanced at the camera. "I don't want to tape this."

Napier grinned, showing him a small wireless remote in the palm of his hand. "Too late. I've been rolling since you walked into the room."

"Welcome to my world," Bill King said.

"For chrissakes." Tom crossed his legs. "Fine. But there are going to be waivers to sign once this is done, and I'm not going to make it easy for you."

Napier gave him a funny look before nodding. "That sounds good to me, Tom. So, just so you're aware, I've got the camera set to a medium shot so the viewer can see I'm sitting on a stool, relaxed and comfortable. It's set at a 25 degree angle so that it looks like I'm looking at you just off-frame. Some people like to shoot just over the interviewer's shoulder, so the viewer knows you're there, but I don't like that look. You're completely out of the frame. All right?"

"Fine."

"So let's hear what you've got."

Tom took a photograph of the assailant from his pocket and unfolded it. "Who's this guy?" He handed it over.

Napier leaned over to take it. He straightened up and gave it a long look. "I think I know him. I can't put a name to it. Is this the guy who's trying to kill me?" He turned the picture around so the camera could see it.

"What does the name Craig Norwood mean to you?"

Napier started. "Craig?" He snapped the picture around for another look. "Good lord, yes. This is him." He was genuinely surprised. "You mean *Craig* is the one trying to kill me? That was *him* at Oxtongue? What the hell?"

"Where do you know this guy from?"

"From when we were kids." He stared at the photo. "In Renfrew. I haven't seen him in years. How long has it been?" He looked away. "Since I left town to go to Simon Fraser. No, before that. I remember hearing he'd dropped out of school and was running with a bad crowd."

He wagged the photograph. "This is going to take a minute to process. Craig Norwood."

"Why's he trying to kill you? He's a hired assassin, Ken.

Who wants you dead this badly?"

"No one! I mean, there's no one hates me *this* much."

Tom crossed his legs the other way. "Let's consider for a moment that he's not on a job, that it's personal. It's a possibility we have to account for."

"It's unbelievable."

"Talk to me about Norwood."

Napier frowned at him. "Talk? Yeah, uh, okay. He was a kid. I was friends with his sister, Sally. I've told you about her before. We horsed around with the Super 8 for a while. Smart kid. Disappeared."

"Only the two kids? Sally and Craig? Or were there more?"

"Just them. Sally was two years younger."

"How well did you know Craig?"

Napier shook his head. "Not all that well. We never played together. He kept pretty much to himself. A loner type."

"You said something about him getting in trouble a lot when he was a kid."

"Yes. Quite a lot. Sally confided in me because she had to have someone to talk to, and she could trust me not to blab it all over the place."

Tom waited.

"Trouble at school, and trouble in town. When he was in Grade Four, I think it was, he set fire to the field behind the school. Our school was on the edge of town, and there was a big field behind it. He set fire to it so we'd all get sent home. He didn't feel like being there that day, I guess. The kids loved it but the teachers and parents were pretty upset. Not to mention the fire department and police. That's one example."

Tom nodded for him to go on.

"He didn't like the teachers. At all. Every now and again

one of them would have a punctured tire. He was caught a few times with a knife. It was taken away from him, of course, but it was like he had an endless supply. Another one would appear in the sheath on his belt, like, the next day."

"And in town?"

"Got caught for shoplifting a couple of times, broke the odd window." Napier made a face. "See, the thing about Craig was that he wasn't a punk. He didn't give off this bad attitude, do you know what I mean? When he was caught doing something, he just went quiet and took whatever punishment they handed out. And because of that, because he was, well, polite and almost well-mannered, they tended to let him off and send him home to his parents with a warning."

"And what did his parents do?"

"That's just it. They did nothing. His dad was an electrician and worked a lot of hours and his mom, I don't know, I think she was a little afraid of him. That's the impression I got. Craig pretty much had free rein to do whatever he wanted."

Tom had been thinking while he listened, trying to build up a picture of a contract killer as a young troubled boy. At some point, he would have killed for the first time. When had that happened?

"Was he violent? As a boy?"

Napier raised his eyebrows. "Oh, he had a quick pair of fists. He was tough. But you know something, I don't ever remember hearing that he was the one who started the fights. For a while, some of the kids badgered him for being quiet and withdrawn, but it tapered off after he pounded the crap out of a few of them. After that, it was just guys who thought they were the toughest in town and wanted to prove it by taking him on. Eventually, that tapered off, too."

"Did he ever seriously hurt anyone?"

Napier looked at the ceiling, trying to remember. "Yeah, now that I think of it. I remember he cut a kid at the hockey arena. They got into a fight in the washroom. I don't remember what came of it. I suppose the kid had to go to the hospital, and the police were called. I wasn't really clued in to a lot of it back then. I had my own little world to think about."

"What was it like between you and him?"

"There was nothing, really. I suppose he cut me a bit of slack because I liked his sister. I don't really remember speaking more than a few words to him the whole time I knew him."

"Why would he want to stop you from writing your book?"

"That's the thing. I have no idea. It's insane. I mention him, I think, once. That's all. There's nothing, absolutely nothing, he'd object to."

"Okay." Tom stood up. "I've got stuff to do." He looked at Bill, who nodded. "Stay here with these fine people and try not to drive them insane. Okay?"

"Sure. As long as you and-or the police get this guy soon so I can go back to my life. I've got stuff to do too, you know."

Tom looked at Elaine. "You all right?"

She nodded unhappily.

"Sit tight. I'll be back."

CHAPTER 40

Tom had only been to Renfrew a few times before, a number of years ago, and his memory of the place was a little vague, so he drove around for a bit to reacquaint himself with the town.

Policed by the OPP, its population of just over eight thousand people was pretty much settled into the small-town, rural mindset typical of many communities fairly isolated from large urban centres and stuck at an average income of just over thirty grand a year.

People either worked in the retail service sector, the hospital, the long-term care centre, or the tape factory that produced some of the best hockey tape and duct tape in Canada. Just ask the Orlando Solar Bears hockey team, who endorsed their hockey tape, or the comedian Red Green, who pioneered the use of their duct tape on absolutely everything and taught us how cars can be repaired and goose sculptures created with this miracle product.

Tom drove past the Stanley Funeral Home, where Ken Napier had grown up. It was a quiet day for them; Tom could see someone washing one of the hearses in the back parking lot.

He thought twice, pulled a U-turn at the next set of lights, and went back.

Inside, he found the main offices and showed Norwood's picture around on the off-chance that he'd been there lately, looking for a lead on Napier's whereabouts. No sale. Everyone was very nice but not interested, since they didn't know anything about Napier, Norwood, or duct tape, for that matter.

Outside, he ran the printout past the guy with the hose, with the same outcome.

"Why you looking for him?" The guy wore black suit trousers, a black vest, shiny black shoes, and a white shirt open at the neck. In his thirties, his black hair was thinning but his arms were long and muscular. Tom thought it notable that he was comfortable washing his car in his good suit. Sort of a Jason Statham-Transporter type of thing to do.

"He's causing a bit of trouble for a client of mine," Tom said.

"Sorry to hear that. Wish I could help."

"Don't worry about it."

Craig Norwood's home was located on a five-acre piece of land on the edge of town. A small pasture fronting the road was fenced off for sheep, and the driveway running up to the house was lined with apple trees in full blossom. It wasn't at all what Tom had expected.

A woman walked out of the barn at the sound of his tires. She was carrying a wire basket filled with eggs and had a small child riding in a harness on her back. She put the basket down in front of the kitchen door at the side of the house and walked up to his car as Tom stopped and shut off the engine.

She was around forty, stout, and her brown hair was cut in a straight bob. The child was small, a girl, with chubby cheeks and the same straight brown hair as her mother. The woman folded her arms and watched him get out of the car.

"Help you?"

"I'm looking for Craig Norwood. Is he here?"

She shook her head. "In town right now. What do you want with him?"

"I'm trying to sell him my dad's old pickup truck. I listed it online and he sent me a message saying he might be interested."

"Liar. I can smell the cop coming off you from all the way over here."

"I'm not police," Tom said. "When do you think he'll be back from town?"

"Soon enough to kick your ass off our property if you stick around any longer."

Tom took out a picture of the assailant, a.k.a. Craig Norwood, and held it up. "Is this your husband?"

She made a face. "Christ, no. He's a lot better looking than that."

"But this is the Norwood residence, right?"

"Of course it is. Did I say it wasn't?"

Tom put the picture away. "All right, I won't argue. I—"

"That looks like some kind of surveillance photo. Where'd you get it?"

"Do you have a photo of your husband, Craig Norwood, that I could see?"

She huffed and sighed before taking out a wallet from her jeans and digging around in it for a folded snapshot. She handed it to him.

It was a photo of a forty-something redhead with freckles and a large mouth. On the back was written: "To Sharon, Love

Craig."

The handwriting was careful and neat. Tom was by no means an expert graphologist, but he'd seen enough samples over the years to be able to make an educated guess that this inscription had been written by a woman, rather than a man. By Sharon Norwood? Was it part of their cover story, a fake husband in place of the real one?

"This is him? Craig Norwood?"

She put the photo back in her wallet. "Yep. Now beat it, mister, before I call the real cops."

Tom looked around the yard, saw nothing warranting further questions, and got back into his car. Out on the road, he drove down a few dozen meters and pulled a U-turn before stopping in front of a gate leading into a field.

It was late afternoon, and Tom figured things would begin to happen fairly soon. He wasn't really sure what he was looking for; he just wanted information. And to send a message. If Sharon Norwood and her husband were in communication, she'd contact him right away to tell him about Tom and his surveillance photograph.

What would Norwood do in response? He would still be unsure of Napier's whereabouts after his failed attempt, but this would tell him where Tom could currently be found.

After ten minutes or so, a school bus appeared in a cloud of dust and discharged two girls, who danced up the driveway to the Norwood house. So, three daughters? They looked about ten and eight. Norwood appeared to have a complete family tucked away here in eastern Ontario. Did his wife know that he was a contract killer? What had the children been told?

He gave it another hour, but no red-headed husband appeared. It was close to suppertime, and Sharon had insisted that his return was imminent.

Satisfied that Craig Norwood was nowhere near this comfortable little farm home, Tom started the engine and drove away.

Whether Norwood was in regular communication with his wife or not, Tom was confident his message would be delivered, no matter if by text, e-mail, or telepathy.

The hunter was now also the hunted.

Chapter 41

When the cellphone that Norwood used to stay in touch with Sharon buzzed, his mind went dark. Something was wrong. She never contacted him; it was always the other way around.

He was on the road, between Selwyn and Peterborough. He found a place to pull over and dug the phone out of the knapsack on the seat beside him. It was a text:

Cop type here. Surveillance photo of you. Got rid of him with a fake pic.

Norwood knew instantly it was Faust. How the hell had he tracked down his real identity? He'd always been so very careful to insulate his home life from his professional one. Cut-outs and false identities and all the rest of it. Was it this phone? Had Faust somehow managed to trace it?

Sharon mentioned a surveillance photo. Had Faust shown it to Napier, who recognized him?

Norwood fought to control the anger spike that coursed through him. The son of a bitch. Another mistake. He'd dismissed Faust as an elderly Wyatt Earp, washed-up and stuck with menial babysitting tasks, but he clearly still had some juice left. Damn it. This outrage was not to be tolerated.

Finally, when his breathing was back to normal and his vision had cleared, he turned his attention back to the phone.

Sit tight. I'll take care of it.

Norwood was accustomed to having complete control over these situations. He was an unseen, outside factor in the lives of his targets. He stalked them, he prowled around the edges of their days and their nights, and when he struck it was a complete shock, a blitzkrieg from out of the blue. Now, suddenly this old goober cop was taking the initiative onto himself and threatening Norwood right where he was most vulnerable. The bastard.

His phone buzzed again:

Are u ok? We need to talk next time your home.

Once Napier and Faust were out of the way, Norwood would have to re-evaluate how he was doing things. Everything. He hated the thought of having to uproot Sharon and the kids to protect them from future threats, but it might be necessary.

All right. Fine. When he was in Belize, he'd check out Yucatán, the Mexican state just north of Belize. He'd heard it was a great place to live—cheap, safe, and with great weather and spectacular beaches. The capital city, Mérida, was said to be the safest municipality in North America. They spoke Spanish there, he figured, but there'd be English as well because of the tourists. Plus, Sharon already spoke French so maybe she could pick up the native lingo too.

He could set up a little carpentry business in Mérida. Hire a bilingual assistant. Cut down on the number of Devoir assignments he'd accept. God knows, after the Belize job was done he'd be set for life in Yucatán, where only $20,000 USD a year could pay for a decent lifestyle.

Of course, Mexico had an extradition treaty with Canada, so if his chickens came home to roost here at home he might have to duck across the border into Belize to wait it out. Sharon had handled so many absences, it would just be one more for her to cope with.

Thinking about a contingency plan calmed him down. This situation was manageable. He just had to maintain his focus, do what he always did, and then he'd be out of it and into a new setup.

Okay, then.

Time for a counter-offensive, Mister Tough Guy Faust.

CHAPTER 42

When Tom used a new pre-paid phone to call Trish, intending to ask her for more background information on the Norwood property and Sharon herself, Trish was greatly relieved to hear his voice. Apparently she'd been trying to reach him without realizing he'd disposed of the last phone he'd used to talk to her.

"What's going on?"

"I just spoke to a man who identified himself as a Mister Harry Wilson. He wanted to talk to you. Does that name ring a bell?"

"No, can't say it does. What did he want?"

"I'll play you the recording."

The line went silent for a moment, and then Trish's recorded voice said, "May I ask what this is about?"

"It's a personal matter; there's been an accident and I need to get in touch with Tom right away."

Tom went completely still, listening. There was no discernible distortion in the voice, no indication that the caller was using an app or device to disguise its sound this time. He was listening to the voice of Craig Norwood. He was sure of it.

"Could you give me a number where I can reach him? He's not answering his cell."

"I'm sorry," Trish replied. "I can't do that."

"Could I leave a message that you could pass on to him? It's urgent."

"What's the message?"

"Okay. This is Harry Wilson; I'm Kelly's cousin. I'm afraid Kelly's been hit by a car, and she's about to go into surgery. I'm here right now at the Peterborough hospital. She was conscious for a few minutes and asked for him. That's why I called, to see if he could come to the hospital right away. I'll meet him at the front entrance."

"Dear me, that sounds terrible. I'll see what I can do to pass on the message, Mister Wilson."

"Thanks. It's very urgent. She's hurt pretty bad."

"I understand."

"Thanks. I've seen his picture, so I'll know him."

The line went silent again, before Trish's live voice returned. "That was it, Tom."

"Thanks." He knew she was dying to ask about it, but was grateful her professionalism kept her quiet.

"I'll take care of it." He ended the call.

There were times in his career when he knew he was about to confront a suspect he very much wanted to get his hands on. The feelings of excitement and anticipation, the tingling in his muscles and the tightness in his stomach, were very much like what a professional athlete experiences when he or she is about to take the field. He felt those emotions now. Time for a showdown.

First, though, he had to take care of personal business.

He called Kelly Reed's number and, as expected, it went

straight to voicemail. He left a message asking her to give him a call later on, leaving the number of the pre-paid phone he was using at the moment.

She was currently in Malmö, Sweden, with her aunt, Nancy Gillespie. Nancy, an urban geographer emeritus, was presenting a paper at the UNIC Thematic Conference at Malmö University. The conference, on urban resilience, sustainability, and the future of inclusive post-industrial societies, was co-funded by the United Nations Information Centres and the European Union. It was being held from May 7 to May 9, and Kelly and Aunt Nancy planned to stay an extra few days to enjoy the tourist experience.

Nancy's paper was entitled "Circular Economies and the need for Urban Refurbishment in Canada." If Tom had to sum it up in a single sentence after listening to the two of them describe it before they left, he'd say it had something to do with Nancy's ideas about fixing problems with garbage in Canadian cities. At least he figured it was something like that.

He was aware, though, that "refurbishment" was Nancy's joke word. She hated fancy rhetoric at the best of times, and she was actually pretty pissed off about the lack of progress in our municipalities. Her suggested approach, as he understood it, was rather more along the lines of a nuclear explosion than genteel refurbishment.

As always, when he thought of Nancy he thought of her twin sister, Alice, who'd passed away a year ago. The two sisters had lived together in a craftsman house on Homewood Avenue in Peterborough, as different as they were inseparable. While Nancy was the geographer, Alice was actually Dr. Alice Gillespie, a professor of mathematics who taught music on the side. She was the nice one, while her sister was the curmudgeon.

A week before Christmas last year, Alice suffered a massive stroke and died the next day. Kelly, who was a registered nurse employed at the hospital, was at her bedside with Nancy when the moment came. They were both heartbroken.

While Kelly had seriously been considering moving in with Tom at the church in Selwyn, she decided instead to remain at Homewood Avenue with Nancy, who was 81 years old and in need of a bit of a hand with things now and then. Nancy became very worked up when Kelly told her she was not going to move out, refusing to take the blame for interfering in Kelly's relationship with a man whom she regarded, incredibly, as a welcome addition to her family.

Tom and Kelly ganged up on her, forcing her to accept the inevitable.

Since then, Kelly and her aunt had travelled whenever she could get time off. It was her way of helping Nancy deal with the grief of losing her twin.

If, for some reason, Kelly had returned to Canada unexpectedly, she would have found a way to let him know. At the very least, she would have left her phone on in the expectation that he would call. Tom was completely confident that Harry Wilson was Craig Norwood, that he'd somehow gotten Kelly's name and learned of her relationship with Tom, and that he was luring Tom to the hospital, where he'd walk right into an ambush of some kind.

War had been declared between them, and this was Norwood's first offensive campaign.

Here we go.

Chapter 43

Tom pulled into the parking lot at the front of the hospital. Luckily, a spot came open as he was circling around, so he quickly put the rental into the slot and got out.

As he approached the main entrance, a man in custodian clothing stepped up. "Excuse me, are you Tom Faust?"

Tom stopped. It wasn't Norwood. "I'm Faust."

The man looked uncomfortable. He glanced at a piece of paper in his hand, which Tom could see was a printout of a newspaper article, comparing the photo in the article to Tom's face. He nodded.

"A Mister Harry Wilson asked me to watch for you while he stepped in to use the washroom. He said to tell you he'd be there. It's just inside on the right."

"Thanks." Tom walked through the sliding doors of the main entrance and looked around. It was moderately busy, with a few patients being pushed in wheelchairs and administrative types with file folders and clipboards walking up and down the wide corridor on their way to some office or other.

On the right was the doorway to the washrooms. Women to the left; men to the right. He went right, and around the barrier into a typical setup with sinks on the left, stalls on the right, and urinals down at the end.

It looked empty. A few steps in, he heard movement behind him. The whisper of rapidly moving feet. A knife appeared over his right shoulder on a diagonal course to his throat.

Tom threw up his hands and pivoted before the guy could get a tight grip on him. It was Norwood. He looked him in the eyes while his hands dropped down onto Norwood's forearm, stopping the progress of the knife just as it began to touch the skin under his jaw.

Norwood strained, muscles bulging, trying to free his arm from Tom's grip, but Tom had physics on his side. Easier to push down, taking advantage of the tyrant gravity, than to pull up against it.

As they struggled, Tom took a step to his right, eyes still locked on his assailant's. He took another step so that his leg was behind Norwood, whose right arm was still wrapped around Tom's shoulder. He pulled his head out from under Norwood's arm and twisted the knife hand behind the man's back.

He drove his knee into the back of Norwood's knee and twisted his wrist as Norwood crumpled. The knife flew across the floor and clattered under a barrier into a stall.

Norwood used his downward momentum to fall into a somersault that pulled him free from Tom's grip. He kept going through another roll, made it to his feet, saw that Tom was between him and his knife, and ran away.

Off balance, Tom dove at his ankles like a football safety trying at the last moment to prevent a touchdown. He missed and banged his chin on the floor.

He lay there for a moment, winded, listening to Norwood's footsteps disappear into the white noise in the corridor.

Finally, he staggered to his feet with some effort and leaned back against the sinks, trying to catch his breath. Twenty years ago, he'd be taking the bastard into custody instead of wheezing like a punctured bagpipe. Hell, ten years ago.

A man emerged from one of the stalls. He was holding Norwood's knife. He put it next to one of the sinks and began to wash his hands.

He dried them under a high-powered blower, all the while watching Tom from the corner of his eye. When his hands were dry and the blower had shut down, he turned and said, "You all right?"

Tom nodded.

"You're bleeding."

Tom looked at his reflection in the mirror. There was a nick just under the point of his jaw on the left side. A trickle of blood ran from the cut, down under his collar. It could have been a hell of a lot worse, he reflected. A lot worse.

"Guess I'd better get a new razor," he said.

CHAPTER 44

Norwood walked briskly out through the sliding front doors. A glance over his shoulder assured him that Faust wasn't hot on his trail. The custodian he'd used to lure the old man inside was putting out his cigarette, his break finished.

"He didn't show up?" Norwood asked, feigning anxiety.

The man looked surprised. "Yeah, he did. I told him you were in the washroom. Didn't you see him?"

"Shit. How did I miss him? Which car is his?"

"The Bronco. I gotta go. Good luck."

"Thanks." Norwood waited until he disappeared inside, pretending to fumble for his phone in his pocket, before strolling down the cement walk into the parking lot. After a moment he spotted the Bronco, in the next row from where he'd parked his Mercedes.

It was empty. He detoured over to his car and got in. He slumped down low in the seat, waiting.

The old guy was proving to be a formidable opponent. Norwood's intention had been to hold the knife to his throat, jockey him into an empty stall, force him to give up Napier's whereabouts, and then slit his throat. He hadn't expected him to be that fast and strong. What the hell was it with cops? They were like something out of *Night of The Living Dead*. Frigging zombies that wouldn't go down.

If Faust came out to his car and drove away, Norwood would follow him and watch for another opportunity to take him down. He waited. Cars left the parking lot and others came in. Finally, a City of Peterborough police cruiser turned in the driveway, light bar flashing. It rolled up to the main entrance. Using the car's mirrors, he watched a uniformed constable stroll inside.

He gave it a few more minutes. The odds were very much in his favour that the cop was there to see Faust, and that the old man would be fully occupied for the next while. Digging into the knapsack on the seat next to him, he took out a magnetic tracking device.

He got out of the car and mooched over to the row where the Bronco was parked. When he reached it, there were no watchers around him, so he swiftly knelt, reached under, and attached the tracker to the undercarriage.

He returned to his Mercedes and left the lot, not wanting to press his luck by hanging around any longer. He drove a few blocks, parked in front of a house with a For Sale sign on the front lawn, and killed the engine.

He used his cellphone to activate the tracker.

Patience is a virtue, he told himself for the thousandth time since he'd started off in this business.

It was only a matter of time before Faust's blood would be spurting onto the ground like water leaking from a balloon with a hole in it.

CHAPTER 45

The nurse looking after Tom cleaned his neck wound and put in two stitches before covering it with a small patch. She used a cotton ball to brush disinfectant on the abrasion on his chin, then used her little finger to smooth down the edge of the patch.

"I've seen the knife," she said. "You were lucky."

Tom grunted. "Maybe if I wear a turtleneck, no one will notice."

The Peterborough constable, whose name was Borden, stuck his head inside the cubicle. "Couple of detectives want to talk to you."

"OPP?"

Borden rolled his eyes.

Tom looked at the nurse. Because she was one of Kelly Reed's co-workers, Tom knew her slightly. She was small and serious-minded.

"I'm all done with you," she said.

Tom nodded. "Send them in, Borden."

It was, of course, Paisley and Leonard. He started them off with his discovery of the assailant's true identity, describing the process by which Trish had uncovered it as "internal Cage Intelligence procedures."

Leonard acted angry and tough because he hadn't passed the information to them right away, but Tom shrugged, saying there hadn't been time.

When Paisley pressed him for evidence that Norwood was Irwin Dessler's killer, Tom got grouchy himself and said that that was their job, not his.

Eventually they let him leave.

The nurse threatened to put him into a wheelchair for a ride down to the main entrance, but he'd been through that once before when he first met Kelly, and he wasn't going to put up with it again. He just started walking and kept on going, out the sliding doors, down the cement sidewalk, and into the parking lot.

He was about to use the remote to unlock the Bronco when he stopped. Norwood had left a while ago and had had plenty of time while Tom was inside to fool around with his vehicle. Would he have rigged it with some kind of explosive device that would detonate when he used the fob or sat down in the driver's seat or started the engine?

No. No, he wouldn't have done anything like that.

He still wanted Napier's current whereabouts, and while Tom had no doubt deeply pissed him off, he'd want that information before wiping Tom from the face of the earth.

He scanned the lot, looking for any suspicious-looking vehicle or someone sitting in their car.

Nothing.

He unlocked his door, got in behind the wheel, and started the engine.

The Bronco was a nice ride, he reflected. The motor was very quiet. The seat was comfortable, and it had a lot of accessories and features that someone who liked driving cars would want to have.

Including a lack of explosive devices, it would seem.

He left the parking lot and drove a block before another thought occurred to him. He pulled over to the curb and shut off the engine. He got out and popped the hatch.

Spencer had very thoughtfully included a go bag in the back of the Bronco when he had prepared it for Tom's use in Lindsay. Tom poked through it, moving aside a change of clothing and a package of new underwear, a box of latex gloves, a folding baton, a zip-lock bag of various kinds of batteries, a pre-paid phone still in its package, until he found what he was looking for—a wireless signal detector.

It wasn't quite as good as his own, which he'd left behind at Oxtongue Lake. Hopefully it had been gathered up by the Cage janitorial crew and would eventually find its way back to him. It had been a Christmas gift from Jeremy Dunaway, although an inadvertent one. At the last company Christmas party they'd had a secret Santa thing where everyone bought a gift and anonymously put it under the tree. As each name was drawn, the person would select a gift for themselves, not knowing who'd bought it. When his turn came, Tom chose a smallish box and, when he unwrapped it, heard a little groan of disappointment from Jeremy as he held up a nice hand-held signal detector-slash-anti-tracking detection instrument. Tom looked it up later and discovered that Jeremy had bought it from the more expensive pages of the spy-gadget catalogue.

The one Spencer had left for him was not bad. It would detect wireless signals from cellphone bugs, hidden cameras, voice recorders and, most importantly right now, hidden GPS trackers. Sure enough, when he ran it around the Bronco, it turned up something attached to the undercarriage at the back. Down on his hands and knees, he spotted it and pulled it off.

A GPS tracker, all right.

He was going to drop it down a nearby drain but changed his mind. He put it back in place. Two can play the ambush game, he thought.

Norwood might know where he was heading, but he wouldn't know what was waiting for him there.

As soon as he got behind the wheel, his phone buzzed.

"Faust."

"Tom, it's me. Is everything okay?"

It was Kelly Reed.

"Slender as a Reed, everything's fine. How's Sweden?"

"Wonderful! Aunt Nancy won't admit it, but I think she's enjoying herself. She found out she likes Swedish food. You know what she's really gone nuts over?"

"What's that?"

"Räksmörgås. It's an open-face sandwich with lettuce, hardboiled eggs, mayonnaise, cherry tomatoes, and prawns. I tried one and it was okay, but she can't get enough of them."

"Sounds . . . interesting."

She laughed. "I—oh drat, she's calling me already."

"That's all right, Kelly. Go see what she wants."

"I wanted to talk to you for a while. Are you sure everything's okay?"

"Positive. I just wanted to hear your voice."

"Sweetheart. Love you."

"I love you, too."

The call ended. He closed his eyes, her voice still echoing in his head, and smiled.

Chapter 46

When Tom reached Omemee, a village of just over twelve hundred people east of Lindsay, he found the abandoned elementary school he'd been looking for and parked in the lot behind it. Leaving the engine running, he called Bill King.

While King was technically in Protective Services and not a field operative per se, he'd cut his teeth in Ops and was more than willing to back Tom's play. Lona Martin would be able to stay at the safe house with Napier and Elaine, assisted by the mysterious Mr. Palmer.

Ending the call with King, Tom called Kate Greene. He was relieved when it went unanswered and forwarded to voicemail. He wasn't sure exactly how pissed off she was with him right now.

"Kate, I'm in Omemee. Your suspect, Craig Norwood, is going to rendezvous with me behind the former Lady Bing Elementary School in Omemee, on Highway Seven. You should call out a team from the Kawartha Lakes Detachment to head over here. Talk to you later."

He sat back to wait on things to develop. His eyes ran around the Bronco's interior with approval. When the job was done, he might pick up one, maybe through Auto Trader or something similar that didn't involve bothersome salesmen. It would be a good second vehicle to supplement his beloved Town Car, something he could use while working.

He knew that Norwood would zero in on him because of the GPS tracker. He wished he had a firearm, like in the good old days when he carried a badge, but he'd manage. Part of his job now as a private investigator was to figure out how to extricate himself from difficult situations without the help of a 9MM SIG-Sauer.

Omemee. How long had Neil Young lived here? The rock-star-to-be was just a kid at that time, between five and ten years old or something like that. The elementary school still operating in the village was named after his father, Scott Young. Tom smiled. As a kid, he'd received copies of Scott Young's novels *Scrubs on Skates* and *Boy on Defence* for his birthday and for Christmas. Somehow they'd gone astray over the years, which bothered him. He'd read them over and over again.

Good memories.

There is a town in north Ontario. . .

That whiny voice that ended up being worth so many millions.

Not Tom's favourite performer. He was far too deep into 1970s progressive rock to have much interest in LA folk rockers. Buffalo Springfield, The Byrds, and the like.

He heard the sound of a car pulling off the highway and swinging around the building.

Show time.

A black Mercedes-Benz pulled up alongside him, and Norwood stepped out.

Tom got out and leaned against the back fender of the Bronco.

Norwood walked around the front of his car and stopped at the top of the gap between the two vehicles. In his hand was a gun, a .22 from what Tom could see, with a suppressor threaded onto the barrel.

No more fooling around, apparently.

Norwood took a few steps closer and stopped, raising the gun.

"That's a Smith and Wesson M & P, isn't it?" Tom said. "Range gun. A plinker."

"You know your firearms, do you?"

"It's been my business for quite a few years. Craig Norwood, I presume."

"Never mind my name. You know what I want."

"Or is it Harry Wilson? Ian MacDonald? Daniel Freeman?"

"Cut the bullshit, Faust. Where's Napier?"

Tom shook his head.

"This can be easy," Norwood said, "or it can be hard. Your choice."

"I don't understand," Tom said, genuinely puzzled. "What's the deal? You're a professional, you've obviously got a track record, but you're acting like a bumbleass beginner. I shouldn't have been able to get within a thousand miles of you, but here we are. What's going on?"

"Look, just stuff the shit and tell me where he is. Maybe I'll let you live."

"Did you kill Dessler because he wouldn't give Napier up?"

The gun chuffed as Norwood shot him in the foot.

Tom went down like a sack of potatoes, his head striking the rocker panel of the Bronco. He pulled up his right leg and tried to grab his foot. "Jesus!"

"Lots of body parts left," Norwood said, looking down at him. "Where's Napier?"

"Jesus, man! Why the hell did you shoot me?"

"Shit, I don't know. Because I felt like it. Because you won't tell me what I want to know. I think I feel like shooting you again. Let's see. . . ."

Tom braced for it.

"Fuck."

Tom looked up. Norwood was looking out at the highway.

"What the fuck?"

Tom rolled and looked under the car. He could see the flashing lights of police cruisers as they approached the school and slowed down.

"Son of a fucking bitch." Norwood gave Tom a swift kick on the side of the head and ran.

Tom was vaguely aware of a slamming car door, an engine revving, and a sudden open space beside him. He heard sirens start up, and then he passed out.

PART THREE

THE FINAL ASSAULT

CHAPTER **47**

When Tom regained consciousness, he was lying on a gurney in a busy hospital corridor. At first his mind was a blank, the sounds and movement around him meaning nothing, but at some point things seemed to snap into place.

Tom Faust.

Napier.

Norwood.

Hospital!

He tried to sit up, but pain surged through his head.

He remembered Norwood's boot zeroing in on his temple. The pain modulated down to a steady throbbing.

He could remember it. Which meant no concussion. No concussion! He'd been down that road before and had no desire to go through it again.

He'd passed out, so it must have been from the pain instead of the kick in the head.

The pain.

His foot!

He tried to sit up again to look at it, but paid the price once more.

A minute or two, just to rest.

The foot was numb. There was no pain. Anaesthetic? He could move his leg, and it felt floppy and weighed-down at the end, so presumably the foot was still there.

He was still dressed in the clothing he'd worn when it happened. Thankfully, they hadn't stripped him and put him in one of those godawful smocks. They'd slit the right leg of his jeans, though, from the cuff to the knee, so they could work on his foot.

Someone passed his gurney with no room to spare, banging his arm. A clipboard sitting on his lap slid over to one side.

Goddamned hospital. Where was this, anyway? Lindsay?

He fumbled for the clipboard and, without raising his head, held it up where he could see it. He didn't have his glasses, so he had to squint.

> *Gunshot wound; infection, no; hallax, six stitches; second metatarsal, four stitches; something-or-other CCs lidocaine; abrasion right temple; patient briefly conscious at admission and exhibited satisfactory recall; no evidence of concussion; protocol recommended; x-ray scheduled for gunshot wound.*

Screw that.

He flipped to the next document, which was a report to the police by the attending physician that was required for all gunshot wounds. It was signed off by Paisley. Had he talked to them? Tom couldn't really remember. He'd probably been unconscious when the detectives stopped by.

"Here you are. I've been looking all over the damn place for you."

Tom looked up at Bill King. "Get me the hell out of here."

"Maybe you should stay until the doctor sees you."

"Bullshit. Help me up." As Bill took hold of his arm, Tom levered himself up into a sitting position on the edge of the gurney. Ignoring the pain, he slid his butt down and put his feet on the floor. One, his right, was bandaged and encased in a walking boot. His sliced pant leg was taped around the top of the boot. The other, which had full sensation, was without a shoe.

He took a step and his knees buckled. Bill reached for him but Tom waved him off. Looking around, he saw that the gurney parked behind his was empty save for a pair of crutches. He limped over and grabbed them.

"Let's go," he said, a four-legged former cop thumping steadily toward the elevators.

When they got outside, he let Bill take his arm to guide him toward the parking lot.

"Where's the client?"

Bill unlocked the doors of a white Ford F-150 pickup truck and helped Tom into the passenger seat. "We moved them. I'll take you there now."

"I hope you've got ibuprofen," Tom said as Bill started the engine.

"Whatever you need."

They drove in silence along Highway 7 until Tom realized they were going to Peterborough.

"You've got a home in this area, don't you?" Bill asked, eyes on the road.

"In Selwyn. A decommissioned church."

"How'd you manage to get that?"

Tom smiled. Well, half-smile and half-wince. "Luck. I was driving along a back country road one day, saw a For Sale sign, and pulled over to take a look. It was in so-so shape, but the stone was good and the foundation was solid. So I took a chance."

"A church. Is it haunted?"

"Not that I know of. Anyway, I play my music loud enough to scare the ghosts away."

Bill laughed. "Stones?"

"Phht. Gentle Giant, Yes, Camel, Nektar, Genesis, Gong; I'm a prog rock guy. Old man music."

"I see."

"So, what about you, Bill? Married?"

"Divorced. Two kids. The split happened when I was in the field." He shrugged. "Too much travelling, too many friends coming around the house when I wasn't there. It's better this way. A lot less stress. You?"

Tom looked out the window. "Linda passed away twenty-five years ago. Plane crash. My daughter was only fourteen at the time."

"That's hard."

"It was." Tom glanced over. Bill didn't seem to know who his daughter was, and that was just fine with him.

When they reached Peterborough, they followed Parkhill Road east, cutting through the north end of the city. A couple of blocks before the canal, Bill turned onto Snelgrove Road, a two-block side street lined with wartime storey-and-a-half homes. He pulled into a driveway second from the end.

Elaine was in the kitchen preparing dinner. Napier, unsurprisingly, was sitting at the kitchen table, typing. Lona Martin was sitting on the couch, reading Salhany's *Practical Guide to Evidence in Criminal Cases*. She put it aside as they came in and helped Tom into the La-Z-Boy. She grabbed a first aid kit out of the closet and began to remove the walking boot and bandages from his foot.

"Bullet passed between your big toe and your second toe," she murmured as she worked. "Right through the narrow space here between the proximal phalanges, the toe bones closest to the ankle."

"It's starting to hurt like hell."

"Did they give you a topical painkiller?"

"Lidocaine."

"Mmm. Short half-life. The bullet tore up the flesh in the triangular area at the top of the toes, see? Removed flesh from both toes."

Tom kept his eyes on a spot on the wall above the TV. He had a decent pain threshold and had seen enough blood to last him a lifetime, but when it came to his own wounds he preferred not to look.

"Stitches are good. No sign of infection, but I'm going to put some topical antibiotic on and cover it for now. You're going to have pain until this heals."

"I guess that's why God invented ibuprofen," Tom said.

"The nerve that services this area," Martin said as she worked, "is called the deep fibular nerve. It runs from the top of your fibula," she tapped his shin under his knee, "all the way down to where you got shot, in the first webbed space on the dorsum of the foot. You'll have to see how it heals. You may walk with a limp from now on, because this nerve provides sensation to the muscles that control your gait and how your foot lifts when you move. If the nerve doesn't regenerate, you could end up with foot drop or some other similar problem. You'll have to be careful what shoes you wear on this foot from now on."

"This is such wonderful news, Martin. Thank you so much."

She shrugged, securing the boot. "The price you pay for enduring a year of pre-med."

She removed the bandage on his neck. "More stitches. You look like you've been run over by a lawn mower."

"Haw haw. Are they all right?"

She cleaned the wound and nodded. "Nice and tight. Just a little messy. Don't want this to get infected, either."

When she was done, Tom stood up.

"You should have crutches," she said.

"They're in the car," Bill said. "Want me to get them?"

Tom shook his head. He limped into the kitchen and started rooting through the cupboards, getting in Elaine's way, until he found a large bottle of ibuprofen. He filled a glass with water and threw down a handful of tablets.

He looked at Napier, who was watching him.

"Are you all right, Tom?"

"I'll live. Bring that laptop into the other room. Time for show and tell."

CHAPTER 48

Norwood was a little drunk. On the way home, he'd stopped at an LCBO and bought a quart of rye, breaking another personal rule. Down at the corner convenience store he picked up a pack of cigarettes, a large bottle of ginger ale, and several bags of pork rinds and cheese puffs.

Back in his condo, he took a long, hot shower. He put on khaki cargo pants and a black T-shirt with the Led Zeppelin cover featuring the Hindenburg dirigible crashing and burning. He turned on the TV, put an *I Love Lucy* disc into the player, poured himself a rye and ginger, and settled back to watch.

Maybe he should cut out for Belize right now. Or to Yucatán, get Sharon and the kids settled there, go down to Belize and do the job, then come back and retire with an extra million U.S. dollars in the bank, just another simple, solitary, white carpenter guy.

But what would he say to Sharon? She didn't know what he did for a living. She had a pretty good idea it was illegal, but he'd always kept the exact nature of his assignments from her. She didn't need to know.

She didn't need to know now, either, but how would

he convince her to leave her little Renfrew hobby farm and permanently move to the Caribbean with him? That it was absolutely imperative? That the whole fucking dirigible was going down in flames?

Goddamn fucking Faust. Goddamned son of a bitch.

He filled his glass, drained it, and filled it again.

As one episode of his all-time favourite television show ended and another began, he took a deep breath and put down the glass. This wasn't like him. He looked at the pack of cigarettes, still unopened. Stress response. He looked at a bag of pork rinds. Another stress response. He grabbed the bag and tore it open.

Mouth full, eyes on the TV, he chewed and thought.

Yes, Mexico had an extradition treaty with Canada. He'd have to destroy everything connected to his real identity and use the family packets Frank Harvey had made for him. Would Sharon agree to assume a new identity? Would the kids? In exchange for an incredible beach, great weather, and cheap shopping? He was willing to bet. Maybe if he got them a place where she could raise a new herd of goats and grow sweet potatoes or whatever.

The thing was, he hated to quit on something. On anything. It infuriated him to think that some old ex-fart was running him off. That Napier would publish his fucking book and expose the one crime Norwood had committed that he'd always regretted. Okay, publish the damned thing. He'd be five thousand kilometers away, impossible to find.

He picked up his glass, drained it to wash down the pork rinds, and smacked it on the table.

No!

He went into his study and brought back his laptop. Tossing

aside the bag of pork rinds, spilling a few on the floor, he booted it up and entered the dark web. Reaching out as Angus Black, he messaged an individual identified only as Fish:

Info needed. Usual fee x 2.

He watched another episode, the one in which Lucy handcuffs herself to Rickie without realizing there isn't a key. It was funny, and it lifted his spirits a little. When the end credits were rolling, his laptop pinged:

At yr service, Blackie. What can I do you for?

Norwood paused. If anyone could tell him what he needed to know, it was Fish. To say that this person was enigmatic would be a gross understatement. No one knew who they were or where they were located. No one knew for sure if they were male or female, gay or straight, young or old, or what race they might be. Everyone knew, however, that Fish was one of the best sources available. At a very high price.

I need an insider at Cage Intelligence Group, Toronto. Someone bought and paid for.

A few moments passed before:

Tough ask. Give me an hour.

Norwood went into the kitchen. He dumped the rest of the rye down the sink and made a pot of coffee. He sat at the kitchen table and drank a cup. He put the bottle of ginger ale in the refrigerator, poured another cup of coffee and wandered back to the couch. It had only been thirty-six minutes, but there was an answer waiting for him.

Teeder7634. Next Door. $$$.

"Next Door" was another network on the dark web where amateurs were allowed to peddle their wares. Norwood seldom bothered with it, not trusting its sellers, but if Fish said this person was the one, then, they were the one.

Another ping:

Cha-chinggg, Blackie.

Norwood chuckled:

My crypto's good, Fish. Thx.

He sent his payment, not regretting the expense, and logged into Next Door. He found Teeder in a directory of vendors and sent them a message:

Info wanted re CIG.

Now, to wait.
But not very long.

CHAPTER **49**

Tom flipped through the channels on the TV and then, annoyed, turned it off. Elaine wandered in from kitchen, a dish towel flipped over her shoulder. She passed Tom's recliner and stood at the window behind him, parting the curtains to look out into the street. Everyone else in the house was occupied with something or other in their own particular world.

"Maybe you should stay away from the windows," Tom said.

She didn't move. Tom thought that maybe she hadn't heard him. Then suddenly she shivered and started to cry.

Tom sat up and turned to look at her. "Are you all right?"

Shaking her head, she knelt down and put her head on his arm.

He was never very good in situations like this, except with Pamela, of course, but when a female began to cry while he was on the job it always made him feel awkward. He usually just let them cry until they were ready to talk about it.

After a while, she lifted her head and met his eyes. "I'm sorry. I don't want to impose."

"Impose? You're not imposing. Talk to me about it."

She lowered her head, but the crying had stopped. She wiped her eyes on the dish towel. "Is Grandpa really dead?"

"Yes, I'm afraid so."

She slowly exhaled. "What happened to him?"

"You don't want to know."

"Yes, I do."

"Look," Tom said, "suffice it to say he was killed by the same person who's trying to kill Ken Napier."

"You mean Grandpa just got in his way?"

"Yes, I'm afraid so."

"So he was collateral damage. That's all he was."

Tom had never liked that term, or the reality that people could be murdered simply because they were in the way. It devalued their lives, reduced them to extraneous cardboard cut-outs in a shooting gallery.

"Where do you live, Elaine?"

She tried to smile. "It's okay, Mister Faust. You don't have to waste your time trying to make me feel better. I'll be okay."

"I'll let you know when I feel like I'm wasting my time. Where's home?"

"Huntsville. I live with my parents."

"What does your father do for a living?"

"Step-father. My father died when I was three. He looked after people's oil furnaces. He had a heart attack in somebody's basement and died there. He was only thirty-seven."

"I'm sorry to hear that. What's your step-father like?"

"Great. He's a really nice guy."

"I'm glad to hear it."

She was quiet for a moment. Then she murmured, "He's really nice to me and mom."

"Tell me about him."

"He's just a little guy. Shorter than me. He's older than mom, but only like five or six years. He's very sweet. Shy."

"What does he do for a living?"

"He's a piano tuner. And, what do you call it, a technician."

"Really."

"Yeah. Whenever there's a concert or show in town, they get him to tune the piano, and he stays for the show in case something happens and they need him."

"Wow."

"Yeah. He gets tickets for mom and me sometimes. We saw George Canyon once. You know, the country music star. Mom really likes him. And Alan Doyle, the guy from Great Big Sea. She likes him, too."

"What about stuff that you like?"

"I don't think Billie Eilish or Taylor Swift are going to make it up to Huntsville any time soon."

"You're a Swiftie?"

"Yeah."

"How old are you, Elaine?"

"Twenty-two. Why?"

"What school did you go to?"

"Huntsville High. Then community college in Bracebridge to do a one-year culinary certificate."

"What was it like to live away from home?"

"Oh, I didn't have to. It's only a half hour away. Mom drove me down and back."

"A culinary certificate. Is that why you like to cook?"

"Yeah, I guess so. I've been trying to get a job in one of the tourist resorts around home, but I haven't had any luck so far."

"Keep trying," Tom said. "I'm sure something will turn up."

She wiped her cheeks with the towel. "Can I ask you a question?"

"Sure."

She looked at him with damp hazel eyes. "Faust's not a very common name."

"No, I guess not."

"Are you related to Pamela Faust, the actress?"

"Yes," he admitted. "She's my daughter."

"Wow, that's really something."

Tom waited for the inevitable autograph request or photo or whatever.

"What's it like?"

"You mean, what's it like to have a daughter in the movies?"

"Yeah. To have a daughter who's made something of herself."

Her tone of voice was still low and flat. Tom realized she was thinking about herself more than Pamela.

"Good. Stressful sometimes. Other times, not."

"Thanks for talking to me." She slowly got up and left the room.

"No problem," he said to the silence.

CHAPTER 50

After a bathroom trip, Tom settled down again in the La-Z-Boy, reclining it so that his foot would be elevated. Lona Martin had told him that elevation would minimize the swelling and maximize blood flow to help it heal.

Napier brought in some kind of box-and-cable arrangement that he used to connect his laptop to the television. When it was up and ready to go, he looked at Tom with a question in his eyes.

"Early stuff," Tom said. "How early can you go?"

Napier shrugged. "I got the camera in '89. I was eleven. I saved everything. About five years ago I had a bit of free time, and I digitized the works. It's all here, from '89 to '98, when I went out to Simon Fraser. The earliest stuff that I shot on the Super 8 is not so good. I picked up a Sony HDCAM in 1997 when they came out. That's better quality, if you want to see some of that."

"I want to see what you shot of the Norwoods."

"That'd be the old Super 8 footage." He opened a menu and navigated to a folder that was subdivided by year. "Sally disappeared in '89. After that, I didn't go around there any more."

"Let's see it."

Napier opened the subfolder labelled for 1989. Inside there were a total of thirty-six files. "Some of these were just me fooling around when I first got it. The later ones are bits and pieces I shot with Sally, the idea being we'd stitch them together into a short film."

"Do you know which ones she's in?"

"Yeah. The file names have her initials in them. See? SN."

"Take me through them."

"All right." The files were listed in chronological order, earliest first. Napier moved his cursor down to the fifth file and opened it.

A young girl, apparently Sally, danced in front of someone's verandah stairs. The colour was faded, mostly reddish browns. She wore a long flowered dress that she held up above her ankles. She spun around, smiling shyly at the camera. There was a bit of sound, mostly air puffing into the microphone. She curtseyed, pirouetted again, and stopped.

Behind her, the screen door opened and a woman looked out. She glared at the girl. "Stop that, or take it somewhere else."

Sally looked at her, crushed, and the shot ended.

"The idea was to edit it to remove her mom. We just never got around to it."

He moved on to the next one. Sally stood under a tree, reading a poem from a book. It was a volume of the collected works of Emily Dickinson. Her high-pitched girl's voice came across clearly:

> *Because I could not stop for Death –*
> *He kindly stopped for me. . . .*

"Shit," Tom murmured.

Napier nodded.

She read a few more verses and then looked up. "Is that okay?"

"Yes," came the voice of young Napier from behind the camera. "Just finish the poem and that'll be good."

She read the rest of it and the clip ended.

"The next one," Napier said, "is a cut version, just of her reading the poem. Without the interruption. I was practising my editing skills. Do you want to see it?"

"No," Tom said.

The next few were medium shots of Sally walking through a field, watching a squirrel climb a tree on the sidewalk in town, and a close-up of her looking off to one side, in a three-quarters shot, trying to appear pensive.

"I was imitating the *nouveau vague* filmmakers at this stage," Napier said.

Tom winced, trying to move his leg to a more comfortable position. "I don't know what that is."

"Sorry. French New Wave. I'd just seen Godard's *Vivre sa vie* and I was struck by how much Sally resembled Anna Karina, who starred in it. The same dark page-boy hair, the same eyes, the same sad face. I wanted to see if we could get some of that on film."

"Sounds like you had a bit of a crush on her," Lona Martin said.

Annoyance crossed his face for a moment before he nodded. "Yeah. I did."

"What's next?" Tom asked.

Napier moved the cursor down to the next file with "SN" in it. "This is a short one. I'm trying to remember. . ."

Sally was sitting on the front steps in front of her house. Her hands were clasped in her lap. This time her dress was long and black, with white lace trimming.

"She was trying out her Emily Dickinson look," Napier said. "Oh, wait. It's this one."

Sally was talking about her pet cat, Katrina, and why she loved cats so much. The front door opened. A boy in his early teens walked out.

"Craig," Napier said.

Tom watched him trot down the stairs past his sister. He was short and a little heavier-looking than he was now, but he had the same buzz cut, the same clenched fists, and the same tough expression on his face.

He raised his middle finger to the camera, mouthed an obscenity, and walked away. The clip ended.

"What a charmer," Lona said.

Bill snorted. "Tough customer."

Napier nodded. "I steered clear of him as much as I could."

Tom reached for the coffee that Elaine had brought in for him while he was watching. "What did you write about him in your book?"

"Practically nothing. There was a lot about Sally in the chapter where I talked about getting started, you know, with the Super 8, but other than mentioning she had an older brother named Craig I didn't really spend any time on him at all."

He frowned. "In fact, I think the only other time was when I wrote about her disappearance and mentioned that Craig was the only person I saw at their house."

"You wouldn't have any film from that day, would you?'

"No. Yes. What am I saying? I had the camera rolling when

I rode up to Sally's house and Craig came out to tell me she wasn't there."

Tom pointed at the directory on the TV screen. "Tell me it's here."

"Well, yes. I'm using it in my film about writing my autobiography." He moved the cursor down to the last file in the subfolder and clicked on it.

The shot opened on the street, moving slowly. "It's my early version of a dolly shot. I had the camera on the front fender of my bike."

The Norwood house, which Tom recognized by now, gradually approached. The bike stopped. Craig was walking across the front lawn on his way to the shed at the side of the house.

"Hey, Craig," Napier called out, "is Sally around?"

"She's gone," Craig said over his shoulder. "No one knows where. Now fuck off out of here." With that, he disappeared into the open door of the shed.

The camera jiggled as Napier got off his bike and unwrapped the duct tape holding it in place. Then the shot abruptly ended.

"Run it again," Tom said.

"I saw it," Bill said. "Did you see it?"

"Let's take another look."

They waited patiently through Napier's opening dolly shot. When Craig entered the frame, Tom grunted. "Pause it there, will you?"

Napier paused it. Craig was staring at the ground, in mid-stride.

"Left leg," Bill said.

"Yeah."

Napier leaned forward. "What? What are you talking

about?"

Bill got up and walked over to the TV. "See?" He pointed at Craig's left leg, which was thrown forward as he hurried across the lawn. "This dark smear?"

"Blood," Tom said.

"What? Blood? What the hell are you talking about?"

Bill tapped the TV. "It's blood. And not his own. Transferred from someone else, right, Tom?"

"Mmm hmm. Did they slaughter any animals, Ken? Chickens or pigs or something?"

"No, they didn't. They didn't keep farm animals."

"Would he have killed Sally's cat?"

Napier got up and pointed elsewhere on the screen. "There she is, in the front room window. What are you trying to say? That Craig killed Sally and hid her body? After all these years, that's what I'm supposed to believe happened to her?"

"He's a professional killer," Bill said. "Maybe she was his first."

"No. It couldn't be." Napier sat down, staring straight ahead. It was the first time Tom had seen him look this way. Deflated; unsure of himself; horrified.

"It's something we need to consider," Tom said. "If it's true, if he killed his sister and covered it up, if he's lived with it all these years, then your writing this book and making a film about it, including footage from that time," he gestured at the TV, "has brought it all back in spades. He's convinced you know what happened, and you're going to write about it, and he knows as well as we do there's no statute of limitations on indictable offenses in Canada. Maybe, ironically, after all his years of killing, this is the only one that could put him away for good."

"But why? Why would he kill her? She was so sweet and innocent. She never said a word to him, never did a thing to cross him."

"That you know of," Bill said.

Tom nodded. "Bill's right. Only Norwood knows what happened that he's so desperate to cover up he's willing to risk his career in a personal vendetta."

"I don't want any of this," Napier said. "I'm going to publish my book and release my film, but I'm willing to take out any mention of him if that's what he wants."

"I think it's too late for any of that now." Tom wiggled his good set of toes so that he wouldn't try to move the injured ones. "The only thing on his mind now is killing the whole damn bunch of us."

CHAPTER 51

Tom was dozing in the La-Z-Boy the next morning, which was Saturday, after a light breakfast of Captain Crunch cereal and coffee. His eyes flew open when someone knocked on the front door.

Bill came out of the kitchen with a pistol in his hand and looked at Tom, who shook his head. Lona Martin appeared in the hallway. She gathered up Napier and Elaine and took them upstairs to shelter in one of the two bedrooms. Tom got to his feet and went to the kitchen door, where he could jump anyone coming into the living room from the front entry.

Holding the pistol behind his back, Bill went to the door and looked through the glass. He opened the door and said, "Christ, Sean, you scared the hell out of us."

"Let me in, Bill. I can't be standing outside all day."

Bill moved aside and Sean Cage walked in. He glanced over his shoulder at Tom, who was still in his ambush position, and walked through to the downstairs hallway. He looked into the kitchen, the spare bedroom, and the bathroom, before stopping at the bottom of the stairs. He looked up, then looked at Bill, who had followed him.

"They upstairs?"

Bill nodded.

"Tell 'em to come down."

He walked back into the living room, where Tom was making his way to the recliner.

"How's it coming, mate?"

Tom shook his hand. "I'll be fine. No problem."

"Any bones broken?"

"Nah. Only a flesh wound."

Cage smiled at the humour. "Bad enough, just the same." He looked around. "Bit of a dump, don't you think?"

"It's all right. I've been in worse."

"Me too, unfortunately."

Bill came into the living room, followed by Napier and Elaine. Napier was carrying his video camera and a tripod. As he was setting them up in the middle of the room, Cage looked at Elaine.

"You're the kid, are you, then? How're you holding up?"

Her eyes went down. "I'm okay."

"We'll look after you, love. Don't you worry."

Napier was finished with his setup. He shook Cage's hand.

"Sean. Good to see you again."

"Yeah. Let's get this over with."

Napier took the chair Elaine had brought in for herself and set it up in front of the window, so that Cage would have the drapes behind him as a back drop. He turned on a lamp and walked around with a light meter. He repositioned the lamp, walked around again, and motioned for Cage to sit down in the chair.

Cage was a small man. His dark hair was shot through with grey. His forehead was lined, and deep creases dug trenches on each side of his mouth. He wore a brown tweed jacket, a white shirt with blue chalk stripes open at the neck, jeans, and brown penny loafers. His eyes were dark and filled with good humour despite the seriousness of the current situation. Although he occasionally made an effort to corral his Cockney accent, for the most part he sounded just like the actors Tim Roth or Michael Caine.

"I thought you didn't like to be filmed," Tom said to him.

"I don't. This is Brenda's idea. Good PR: that sort of bullshit." He slumped down in the chair.

Napier pinned a wireless microphone on Cage's shirt, shifted the lamp again, walked around, and pronounced himself satisfied. He started the camera rolling, ran through his preliminaries, then gestured for the replacement chair Elaine had brought in for herself. She meekly handed it over and leaned against the door frame as Napier got comfortable next to his camera.

Cage crossed his legs.

"I'll do a voice-over intro later," Napier said, "so we don't have to do all that now. But I'd like you to talk a little bit about your beginnings, if you don't mind. Where were you born and raised?"

"Just so we're clear. I answer your questions, then you answer mine."

"Oh, sure. So, where are you from?"

"Ever heard of Bethnal Green?"

"Tell us about it."

"It's in the East End of London, famous for its bloody mulberry bushes. As working class as you could get, back then, and plenty of brown faces around." Cage inhaled through his teeth. "Demographics aside, which I thought was great, by the way, it's notorious for having been the stomping grounds of Jack the Ripper, that and Whitechapel."

"Oh. I didn't know that. Were you aware of the history of Jack the Ripper when you were growing up?"

"Nah, not really. Too busy trying to stay alive."

"Was it that dangerous?"

"Hold on. Time for my question. Why does this guy want you dead so badly that he's going to all this trouble?"

"He's a contract killer," Tom interrupted, "but we figure his first murder was his sister, when they were kids. We think Ken accidentally filmed evidence of it at the time, and Norwood wants to make sure it doesn't see the light of day."

Napier panned the camera from Cage to Tom and back again.

"Is he willing to negotiate?" Cage asked. "Destruction of the evidence in exchange for backing off on Napier?"

"You've got to be kidding!" Napier exclaimed.

Cage ignored him, waiting for Tom's answer.

"To be honest with you, Sean, I didn't have time to ask him. I was too busy trying to stay alive."

Cage exhaled through his teeth; his version of an amused chuckle. "Fair enough. Is it a step we should consider?"

"No!" From Napier.

Tom shook his head. "I agree. First of all, if he murdered his sister he needs to be brought to justice for it. Second, he's too far gone to be thinking logically right now. His mind is set on killing Ken and me, and that's all there is to it."

"Do you think he's psychotic?"

Tom took a moment to think about it. "You know what they say. A lot of bad guys don't think of themselves as abnormal. They think of themselves as regular guys with good qualities who happen to operate outside of society's rules. In his case, I don't think Norwood's a psychopath. He's just a guy who doesn't respect life and fear death and criminal justice the way the rest of us do."

"All right," Napier snapped, "now that we've answered your question, let's get back to mine."

"Right. Little Seany-boy the East Ender. What would you like to know?"

"You implied it was dangerous growing up. How dangerous?"

"Implied, nothing. I spent a lot of my time in the streets and had more than a few scrapes. But I've always been good at making friends, and that was what sometimes got me out of tight corners."

He leaned forward, clasping his hands between his knees. Napier calmly adjusted his shot.

"There were a lot of Bangladeshis on our street when I was a kid. My best friend was Abdul Hasnat Bagchi, the middle child of a Bengali family of six. I spent a lot of time hanging around their house. They were nice people. I was there so much I picked up a pretty good understanding of Sylheti, which his mom spoke, and Bengali, his da's jabber. They were the first two languages I learned after Cockney."

"What were your parents like?"

"My da was a bartender. He worked in a club owned by the Krays."

"Who?"

Cage leaned his head to one side and glanced at Tom. "Children these days. Don't you remember the movie, Kenneth my boy? Starred the two brothers from Spandau Ballet?"

Napier looked embarrassed. "Yes, of course."

The Krays were celebrity thugs in Bethnal Green," Cage said, "two brothers and their loving mother. Ran a gang known as The Firm. Anyway, da got caught in a shoot-up outside the club when I was eight. That was that."

"Did you—"

"My turn." Cage looked at Tom. "Where's your mind at, bud? Feel like sticking this through, or would you rather head for a beach somewhere and let that flesh wound heal up with some Caribbean salt surf?"

"I'm not going anywhere."

"That's what I thought." Cage slouched down further in his chair. "Our client," he said to Napier, "Mister James Allan Gould, president and chief executive officer of Sloan and Gould, your esteemed publisher and Brenda's friend, suggested to me that I make some roster changes for him. Thought I should shove Tom out and bring in a fresh body. That's how he put it. 'A fresh body.' One that's not bleeding, I suppose."

"I'm not going anywhere," Tom repeated.

"That's right, you're not." Cage surged forward suddenly, pointing a finger. "You've seen this guy, you've talked to him, you've got experience coming out the spout dealing with this kind of killer, and I'm supposed to just toss you aside because you've got a sore foot? I don't bloody think so."

"I appreciate the vote of confidence, Sean."

"Yeah, well, we need a new plan. I don't expect you to be leaping over hedges after this guy, but I want you here using this"—he tapped his head—"to figure out how we take him down before anyone else gets hurt."

He rolled his eyes. "Besides, Brenda's in a state. She thinks you're the dog's bollocks, and there's no way she'll let me pull you out now. So."

He tipped his head at Bill. "Do we need to move these two?"

"I wouldn't say so," Bill said. "Our safe houses are pretty safe."

"You got that from your boss. Our wonderful Bryan Weir thinks the sun rises and sets on his spendid works."

"Maybe a few extra resources," Tom suggested.

"Doing what?"

"Set up a soft perimeter," Bill said. "Monitor activity in the area and report to me. It's a quiet neighbourhood, so anything at all might be something."

Cage nodded and threw himself up out of the chair. "Right, then. I'll have a word with Master Weir. On with it."

"I have more questions," Napier said, annoyed that his interview had been steered off the rails.

"Submit them in writing to my secretary, and I'll get back to you." He stopped and glared in mock severity. "Don't submit them to my wife, or there'll be hell to pay."

He winked at Tom, who'd been the real reason for his visit after all, and disappeared out the front door.

Chapter 52

Norwood was dozing in bed when his cellphone chimed with a message. Switching on his bedside light, he picked it up and saw that he'd received a notification from the dark web. He glanced at the clock: 2:36 A.M. on Saturday morning.

Sighing, he threw off the covers and scuffed into the study. While he waited for the laptop to boot up, he went into the kitchen for a glass of ice water.

Thus hydrated, he slipped into the darknet and logged on, navigating to Next Door where, sure enough, Teeder7634 had sent him a message:

Flat rate $10k. $2k deposit up front.

Norwood snorted, typing:

No deposit until you provide proof of access.

He had to wait a while for the response, long enough to drink his water and fetch another glassful from the kitchen.

Subject of query?

The guy was cautious, Norwood could see. Probably scared to death that he was going to betray internal secrets.

Tom Faust.

This time the response was brisk:

State your question with $1K deposit up front.

Clearly an amateur, Norwood decided. He arranged the transfer of the grand, then typed his question:

What are current locations of Tom Faust & Kenneth Napier?

A long hesitation this time, before:

Peterborough. Pay balance owing now to receive street address.

Christ. What a pain in the ass this guy was. Norwood sent him the rest of the money. It was chicken feed, anyway; he would have paid a lot more to know where his targets were hiding out. Finally:

Safe house. 748 Snelgrove Road, Peterborough.

Norwood cut the connection. If the address turned out to be bogus, he'd go back to Fish and demand compensation. Preferably the guy's actual identity, so he could take him to a motel he knew for a little chat.

If it turned out to be accurate? Well, then.

It was game on.

CHAPTER 53

Norwood went back to bed and slept until mid-morning. After a run, a shower, and a quick breakfast, he sent a message to another friend and worked on Sophia's rocking horse while he waited for a response.

He'd finished sanding the rockers and was now gluing parts together. While the glue was drying, he was cutting pieces of leather to size for the harness, hooves, and trim. As always, it was calming, relaxing work. It reminded him of what it was supposed to be like to be normal. Maybe he could have been normal, if things had gone differently. Who knew.

If he hadn't blown it that day with Sally, hadn't lashed out and—

He set aside his scissors and sipped his coffee.

He was tired, so his thoughts began to wander.

His favourite job? It had to be Itasca State Park, in Minnesota. Located at the headwaters of the Mississippi River, the area was known for its pine forests. Norwood had always liked pine trees. He had a stand of white pine on his place in Renfrew, and he liked the sound of the wind hissing through the branches, reminding him of ocean surf.

With this sound in his ears, he'd stalked and murdered a twenty-year old graduate student from North Dakota State University who was on a week-long field trip in the park. The kid's name was Carter Johnson. He was a geology major who was staying alone in the Clubhouse, a dormitory-style facility featuring a rustic common room with a large fireplace and a screen porch.

Norwood arrived while Johnson was on his second day. Treating himself, since the contract called for an additional ten grand for expenses on successful completion of its terms, Norwood booked himself into Douglas Lodge, a beautiful resort on the lakeshore. This way, he could avoid bumping into the target while at the same time surveilling him to study his movements and tendencies.

Two days later, in the early morning, Johnson set off along a hiking trail into the woods. He stopped several times to forage for rocks and stones, and gradually began to fill his knapsack with specimens. When he reached a slight clearing with a bench, he stopped, removed his knapsack, and drank a bottle of water. Then he shrugged back into the knapsack and began the next leg of his hike.

Norwood casually closed the distance between them. Johnson turned around, hearing his footsteps. Norwood waved lazily. Johnson waved back and promptly forgot about him. Norwood came up to within two meters and put a bullet into the back of his head.

The kid went down without a sound. Norwood rolled him over with his foot. Johnson's eyes were open and lifeless. Norwood rolled him back and headed for the lodge. Job done.

He'd used a .22 Ruger, a range gun, to vary his modus operandi so as not to be strictly a knife and garrotte guy. These weapons had minimal firepower, but .22 rounds had a tendency to rattle around inside the skull like a metal bean in a gourd, wreaking all kinds of havoc to tissue, blood vessels, and brain matter.

The contract earned him $200K USD, plus the expense money, making it a middle-of-the-road deal and nothing too big to shout about, but he'd loved the park and the food they'd served in the lodge restaurant. He was there three days altogether and loved every minute of it.

The kid turned out to be a confidential informant for the police on campus at NDSU. He'd been arrested trying to sell hash to an undercover cop and had flipped on his friends and customers.

The main problem, apparently, was that one of his friends, the guy supplying him with product, was the son of a Mexican Mafia boss controlling much of North Dakota's oil patch. The father put the contract out across the darknet in order to protect his kid from arrest and prosecution.

It was Norwood's favourite job because the target was low-hanging fruit, requiring minimal effort. It was simple and uncomplicated. More than that, though, he'd loved the park and the food, the fresh air, and the warmth of the sun in the early afternoon as it broke through the gaps in the pine forest.

If he didn't have a hard-and-fast rule about never returning to the scene of a job, he'd have taken the girls down there every summer for a week in the lodge.

And another thing—

His laptop pinged.

Finally, the answer he'd been waiting for. He could have what he wanted.

All of it.

CHAPTER 54

Norwood slowed as he reached the side entrance of
a cluster of commercial buildings on Fuller Road in Ajax. It
had rained overnight, and his tires splashed through puddles
and hissed on the pavement as he turned in and rolled slowly
through the yard around the buildings.

This neighbourhood was dominated by industrial facil-
ities. There were car dealerships, a heating, ventilation and
air conditioning (HVAC) manufacturer, a building truss
manufacturer, a chemical wholesaler, an auto collision garage,
and an aircraft landing gear manufacturer, to name a few.

The strip of buildings that Norwood circled included a
transmission shop, an auto paints outlet, a food supplier, and a
car detailing business. Some of the places were closed because it
was Saturday; the others seemed only mildly busy.

He ran along the back of the strip until he came to the rear
entrance of a hunting and fishing supplies wholesaler. He swung
around, shifted into reverse, eased up to their loading dock, and
shut off the engine.

The steel entry door at the top of a short flight of stairs was
propped open with an old paint-flecked boat anchor. A man sat

on a kitchen chair, tilted back against the wall, smoking the stub
of a fat cigar. His legs were crossed. Balanced on his knee was a
quart of Jamaican rum.

"You must be Black." His voice was a rough baritone. He
stared at Norwood through watery blue eyes.

"And you must be Mister Crosby."

"Birdman. I got your message."

"You said you have everything I need."

"Sure do. Everything you want. Not sure if you need it."

Norwood grunted, not in a mood to be cross-examined.

Birdman slowly got to his feet. He was big, bigger than
Norwood. Six-two or three, 230 or 240 pounds. Early sixties.
Thinning, tawny hair sticking up from a speckled scalp. A
chevron moustache, damp with beads of rum. Dirty jeans; dirty
Harley-Davidson T-shirt.

He led the way inside. The place was a typical wholesale
operation, with metal racks filled with fishing rods and shelving
units stacked with cartons containing reels, nets, and supplies.

Something fluttered over Norwood's head. He ducked.

Birdman laughed. "That was Pete. He's saying hello."

Norwood straightened up slowly and looked around. The
place was filled with birds. Parakeets, from the looks of it, and a
couple of white cockatoos. There was a lot of cheeping, fluttering,
and chirping. They all seemed excited to have a visitor, flying
from rafter to rafter for a better look at him.

Birdman opened a door and, flicking on a light, led the way
down a set of stairs to a basement that was as immaculate as a
lawyer's waiting room. Norwood could feel the gentle kiss of air
conditioning on his face. The temperature was normal, neither
too warm nor too cool, and there was no trace of dampness. The
lighting was excellent.

Birdman opened a panel that held a floor-to-ceiling display of fishing lures and flies. Behind it was a heavy-duty metal door and a biometrics station. Birdman submitted to the iris and thumbprint readers. The red light over the door turned green. He opened it and led the way inside.

"Your list is a little unusual," he said.

Norwood walked directly to a table at the centre of the room covered with weapons.

"Your references are sterling," Birdman said, "but I was led to believe you were mainly a knife guy."

Norwood picked up a rocket launcher, an M72A5-C1, the same model as the ones currently supplied to Ukraine by the government of Canada. They were a single-use, pre-loaded weapon, armed with a 66mm explosive anti-tank rocket. He checked the rear cap, which was secure, as was the safety pin, and he examined the exterior tube for cracks: none. The front cap was also good. He'd never fired one before, so Birdman walked him through the basics.

Satisfied, Norwood put it down and picked up an AR-15 assault rifle and tried the heft. It felt good. There were six extra magazines taped together that went with it. Next was a Glock 9mm handgun, with four extra magazines. A pair of combat boots and flame resistant coveralls, in the sizes specified.

"The suitcase is on the house," Birdman said. It was a typical black roller bag, and Norwood would use it to transport his purchases. First, though, came the payment.

While some suppliers dealt in cash, Birdman preferred crypto, so Norwood took out his phone and did the honours. When Birdman nodded, Norwood packed up his stuff and left.

As he hit the 401 eastbound and set the cruise control to 110 KPH, he began to work through his plan.

Chapter 55

Sean Cage had a car and driver, both of which were retained on a yearly contract. The car was a BMW 530i sedan, metallic blue, with rear tinted windows, illuminated kidney grilles on the front, and all the bells and whistles you'd expect on a luxury business vehicle. The driver was one of Bryan Weir's men, Edward O'Neill, whom Cage called Ned. Ned was on his third one-year contract with CIG, and seemed content with the gig.

Cage had pretty much gotten over his discomfort at having been subjected to yesterday's on-camera interview. He had been able to assure Brenda he'd conformed to her wishes, and he'd decided to tell Napier later that it was all classified information that couldn't be released, or some sort of nonsense like that, and then forget about it.

He was on his way to a meeting with a corporate client in the financial services sector where anonymous tips of theft were being investigated internally before turning the matter over to the authorities. He had a small team in place, including Kashi Chopra, one of his best behavioural profilers, and ex-military man Charlie Danko, who now worked in their corporate security section. The three of them were scheduled to meet with Annabelle Poutras, their client, who was executive vice-president and chief legal officer. Kashi had a suspect, and they wanted to present the information to Poutras for a decision on how to proceed. The meeting was being held on a Saturday to take advantage of the relative quiet in the client's executive offices. The company was a repeat customer, which always inclined Cage toward generosity with his time.

Inevitably, his mind cast back once more to yesterday. He hated cameras, and he hated talking about himself. Thankfully, he hadn't been required to answer questions about his entry into the world of intelligence through MI6, otherwise known as SIS, the Secret Intelligence Service. MI6 was the United Kingdom's agency that supplied the British government with its foreign intelligence. As opposed to MI5, Military Intelligence, Section 5, which looked after domestic intelligence, counter-terrorism, and other internal stuff.

After his father's murder, his mother disappeared with his sister, and he never saw them again. Left alone, his tenth birthday due in a week, he was forced to fend for himself. He couch-surfed here and there, as his Bangladeshi friends watched out for him.

Being a determined kid, he stayed in school. His grades remained high enough that he received bursaries to attend the East End School of Science, a Sixth Form academy, where he studied mathematics and physics. Math and physics! Who'd have thought that the scrawny little orphan from an upstairs flat on Chambourd Street would have a brain in his head after all?

Most of his classmates were brown and black, and many became his friends and associates in the dark game of survival in the East End.

At age 18 he was offered university scholarships but, being hard-headed and worldly, he turned them down and accepted an offer from MI6 for a summer internship based on economic hardship. He was an exemplary intern, at least so he was told, and when the term was up he applied for a job. It was suggested to him that he also apply to MI5, but he didn't give it a moment's thought. He knew he'd end up spying on his friends if he took a job with them, and there was no way he would ever do that.

He was quickly hired as a data analyst with MI6, but it wasn't long before he talked his way into field work. After bouncing around for a few months, he was assigned to a job as an intelligence officer in Bangladesh and India, taking advantage of his linguistic abilities and affable nature. He worked there from 1993 to 1997.

In 1997, age 25, he complained internally about Operation Mass Appeal, an SIS disinformation campaign designed to spread false news stories about Saddam Hussein's build-up of weapons of mass destruction in Iraq. Cage hated the dishonesty and what he considered the immoral manipulation of the media, and he made a bit more noise about it than perhaps he should have.

As a result of his mouth, he was sent to Canada as a liaison between MI6 and CSIS, which at the time was not much of a player in international intelligence. He did what he could to help them develop standard operating procedures and what not, but it was pretty much a gulag for unpopular assets such as himself. However, he remained in Canada so long he ended up deciding he liked the place, after all.

Especially after he met Brenda, in 2003.

Born and raised in Toronto, she was a little whirlwind who

swept Sean right off his feet. Her parents having emigrated from Monmouthshire, Wales, she'd inherited a few Welsh stereotypes, including a lovely singing voice (she belonged to a church choir in downtown Toronto) and a visceral dislike of the English. Cage met her at an art gallery in 2003, where she was curating an exhibit of magic realism. He was 31; she was 33. Cage made fun of the stuff, and she combusted spontaneously at the sound of his Cockney accent before even considering his words.

Once she realized he was ridiculing her work, she took up the argument with vigour and venom. As soon as they saw they were gathering a crowd, they put a bookmark in it and agreed to resume the debate later over dinner. Things progressed quite naturally from there.

In 2010, Cage came in contact with Meridian Intelligence Services, a private sector company owned by Derek Winter and Natalie Stone, a husband-and-wife team well known in the community. Winter was a former investigator with the RCMP, and Stone was a former superintendent with the OPP.

In 2012, Cage resigned from MI6. He then made Winter and Stone an offer they couldn't refuse, and he renamed the company Cage Intelligence Services. He retained Winter as company president and Stone as VP of North American Operations.

He then hired Nicholas West, one of his few remaining friends from MI6, to serve as VP of Intelligence, based in London. Unlike Cage, West had maintained good relations with UK intelligence and would be able to negotiate on Cage's behalf when contracts came up for bid.

It was a good company, Cage reflected. Rock solid. They were making money hand over fist. And his senior people had a good eye for recruits. Take Faust, for example. Natalie Stone had fastened on him after his retirement from the OPP, and he had proven to be a valuable resource.

Cage came out of his reverie and saw that they were downtown, edging toward the Brookfield Tower on Bay Street. High-rise office buildings always made him think of 9/11 and the intelligence breakdown that had failed to prevent the attack. Oh sure, the CIA had had an Osama Bin Laden unit—

His cellphone began to ring.

He looked at the call display. "Cage."

"Hi, Uncle Sean. Have I caught you at a bad time?"

"Never a bad time, Trish. Just daydreaming while Ned drives me to a meeting. What can I do for you?"

Ned caught his eye in the rear-view mirror. Cage winked. Ned nodded back and put in a pair of ear buds.

"I picked up something this morning during a routine scan," she said.

"Something not routine, I gather."

She tittered. A little nervously, Cage thought. "No. An unauthorized entry into our system. Late last night. Quite late, actually."

"How late, Trish?"

"Two thirty-nine A.M. Duration, eight minutes and forty-one seconds."

"What were they doing?"

"Accessing files. Including Napier's."

Cage was quiet, digesting that one.

"Quite a few records were opened," she went on.

"All right," Cage finally said. "You're the analyst. What happened?"

"I'm not sure yet. I expect they opened some of them just to distract us from the one in particular they wanted to look at."

"A standard dodge," Cage agreed.

"All the investigations are sensitive. It could be any of them. I wanted to inform you right now about the intrusion."

"Who else knows about it?"

"No one except you, me, and the intruder."

"Make sure it stays that way."

"Yes, Uncle Sean."

"I keep telling you, call me *sir*."

"Sorry, Uncle Sean. Talk to you later."

CHAPTER 56

This time, Norwood took an extra day to surveil the house where Napier was holed up with Faust and his protection detail.

He spent an hour scouting around the immediate neighbourhood and found a three-storey apartment building on Parkhill Road, just around the corner from the target house, that had a vacancy on the top floor at the front. The lock on the apartment door was a breeze to pick. He checked the hydro and found it was still on. Even better, a fridge and stove remained in the kitchen, both working. Jackpot!

Because Snelgrove Road was only a two-block street in a quiet neighbourhood close to the Trent Canal, he was wary of being noticed. He bought a bunch of stuff at the Costco to help him handle the situation, using a membership card belonging to Terry Wallace, the identity he'd assumed for this leg of the mission.

It was busy, being late Saturday morning, but he took his time. He blended in with the crowd, moseyed along, and enjoyed himself. It was kind of fun, shopping. Mindless; stress-free because he didn't give a damn; a brief lark in consumerland with its myriad products, colourful packaging, and tempting deals.

Fun.

He filled his cart with stuff he needed for the mission, and added extras like a case of Mountain Dew, a huge bag of salty popcorn, submarine sandwiches in blister packs, and other various provisions to get him through tonight and tomorrow. He also picked out a variety of magazines to read, including a couple on home renovation, an issue of *Car and Driver,* and several magazines dealing with pottery and ceramics, because he'd been considering adding this line of work to his portfolio of cover identities and wanted to get a feel for it.

He preferred magazines to reading articles online because he needed to minimize his time on the smart phone. Magazines were off the grid, they couldn't be tracked in any way, and they could be thrown in the garbage anywhere without attracting attention.

Much better than a pile of cigarette butts at the corner of a sidewalk to mark where someone had staked out a doorway down the street.

He carried all his purchases up to the apartment he'd commandeered and set himself up. There was no furniture, so he arranged everything on the floor. He turned on his new laptop, connected to the Internet with a USB gizmo, and downloaded software for his new toys. He charged the batteries on his external surveillance cameras, launched the application that ran them, and tested them all. Ten cameras; ten up and running.

He stood at the front window and looked outside. From here he had a view of the intersection of Parkhill and Snelgrove. He watched for half an hour and saw no traffic whatsoever either turning down Snelgrove or turning out onto Parkhill.

Fine.

He left the building for a quick reconnaissance. Down Snelgrove one block; east on Juliet Road and around the horseshoe onto Swanston Avenue; west down to Snelgrove; north past the target house and back on up to Parkhill and his crow's nest. A quick loop.

Absolutely quiet. He had to admit that it was an excellent safe house. Small and compact; on a good street for surveillance; decent exit points in case of an emergency.

He waited until dark, reading one of the pottery magazines. It didn't seem like a particularly difficult skill to pick up, as long as you were good with your hands and had the proper equipment and tools. Once he was set up in Yucatán, he'd give it a try.

When darkness fell, he filled his knapsack and slipped outside.

One of his favourite tools for outdoor work was a battery-powered nail gun that he'd tinkered with until it was virtually silent. The street was heavily treed, and when he reached a spot directly across the street from the target house, he secured one of the cameras to a maple tree. He flicked it on, took out a tablet with the camera software on it, and gave it a test.

A perfect frontal view of the house.

He continued on down to the corner and across the street to a tree that gave a clear view of the intersection, with the target house at the top right corner of the frame. The nail gun spat twice, and another working camera was in place.

He moseyed up Swanston until he was across the street from the house whose backyard was contiguous with the target house's yard. It was another wartime home almost identical to the target house. He watched it for twenty minutes. The lights were off upstairs. A faint light flickered in the front window, suggesting a television set. When he was satisfied that the residents were settled and occupied, he strolled across the street and up their driveway.

No dogs barked.

Their garage gave him a perfect place to attach a camera with a full view of the backyard of his target. The nail gun spat again. He checked the camera; it was fully operational.

Since he wanted a 360-degree view of the house, he decided the best way to do it was to continue on into this yard. He stood under a mature apple tree and verified that he could see the north side of the target house from here. He noted that there were two windows on this side, one upstairs and one downstairs. A fourth camera went up, and he was done.

He crept out to the sidewalk and strolled up the two blocks to Parkhill Road. Back in his apartment, he used the laptop to study the recordings that the system had made so far. He watched himself move from point to point around the circle of surveillance as he set it up. He saw nothing out of the ordinary.

He was particularly interested in the view from across the street on Snelgrove as he walked past the house. Did the curtains move? Were there shadows shifting behind them?

Nothing. If they had external surveillance of their own set up, he had to hope he hadn't presented himself as anything unusual to them.

He grabbed a Mountain Dew from the fridge and the bag of salty popcorn from the kitchen counter. Returning to the living room, he sat down on the floor with his back against the wall, pulled the laptop close, and settled in for a few more hours' surveillance.

CHAPTER 57

Norwood watched the place all day Sunday and all day Monday. To the average person it would have been excruciatingly boring, but he was used to it as a routine and was able to keep his brain occupied so that it didn't start racing around like a caged hamster on a wheel.

He kept both his laptop and his tablet in front of him. He watched the tablet for its real-time display, shifting from camera to camera in a loose routine. At the same time, he kept the laptop on a display of all four cameras at once in a grid. It gave him something else to put his eyes on, but it also provided him the opportunity to catch movement peripherally in one of the frames, as well as to replay sequences without disrupting the real-time feed on the tablet.

He drank Mountain Dew and munched on popcorn, ate subs at meal times, and read his magazines. He kept a notebook of his observations and he dog-eared magazine pages for later reference.

As far as vehicles were concerned, he only saw one, a white late-model Toyota Rav 4 that was parked in the driveway along the side of the house. On Sunday afternoon, two women exited the back door and drove off in the car. They were gone for almost two hours, and when they returned they had quite a few shopping bags to take into the house.

After that, it was quiet.

Several times, through the cameras covering the backyard, he saw a man step outside for a smoke on the verandah. He was middle-aged, a bit heavy, and a bit balding. Norwood didn't know him, but he had the look of a Cage operative.

Through the camera down at the corner, he saw a black Chevy Suburban cruise by. It circled up around Juliet and turned right, rolling up to Parkhill, where his other camera saw it turn left onto Parkhill and disappear out of the frame.

Twenty minutes later, almost to the second, a silver Toyota Corolla took the same route through the neighbourhood. Five minutes after it disappeared, a Ford Escape turned off Parkhill onto Snelgrove and drove the whole two blocks, passing the target house before turning right and disappearing.

Thirty minutes later it was the black Suburban again, turning onto Snelgrove from Swanston, passing the target house, and running up to Parkhill, where it vanished.

Then the Escape. Then the Corolla. Then the Suburban once more.

Then nothing for several hours. Two of them, the Corolla and the Escape, were parked on the side streets where his cameras could see them. The other one, the Suburban, must have gone to ground a block or two away.

A three-vehicle detail, Norwood thought. Maintaining a soft perimeter around the house. Interesting. The Suburban was probably the command vehicle, the one in contact with the team inside.

Time for a little improvisation.

He ran a quick Google search and found a gardening centre that was only a kilometer east of his present location. They opened at eight A.M. tomorrow morning. There was also a convenience store just a few blocks away. He passed the time making a shopping list.

He decided to make his final shopping trip early in the morning, shortly after the stores opened, and then spend the day making six IEDs, improvised explosive devices, two for each intersection.

By the end of tomorrow, he should have gathered enough information to know their routine and be able to plan for an attack early Tuesday morning. At dawn.

It was now dark. Norwood felt a little tired. He rolled out his sleeping bag, crawled in, and slept.

Chapter 58

Tom chafed as the weekend unwound, disliking the necessity of remaining in a defensive mode when there was a son of a bitch running around out there who needed to be caught.

Bill was busy co-ordinating the external perimeter team. Napier spent hours at the kitchen table editing film footage on his laptop. Elaine was talking to Lona Martin, probing her for career advice.

It was Monday. Tom mooched around the house, bored out of his skull. Rummaging through the front hall closet, he was surprised to find amongst the boots and ski poles and jackets, tucked in the back corner, a cane. He pulled it out and looked it over.

It appeared to be oak, with a carving of a lion's head on the handle and a brass tip. He tried hobbling around with it. It was a good length for him, and the handle fit comfortably in his hand.

"Whose place is this?" he asked Bill.

"Ours. Cage's. We own all our safe houses." He looked at Tom. "Safer that way."

"Who's Mister Palmer? In Lindsay?"

"Don't be nosy."

Tom smiled indulgently. "Okay. What about all the stuff in here?"

"I don't know. Came with the house, I guess. Probably an estate sale or something."

"I'm going to requisition this," Tom said, holding up the cane.

Bill looked it over. "Very nice. Looks antique. Don't like the crutches, eh?"

Tom made a rude noise.

"Well, help yourself." Bill turned back to his comm centre as someone reported in.

Tom took his prize back to the recliner and stretched out. He fell asleep with it lying across his lap.

They woke him for dinner. He ate in the recliner, on a tray that Elaine brought out and took away again later, although he hadn't eaten much. Dessert was ibuprofen.

When she'd loaded the dishwasher and finished tidying up, she came into the living room with Tom and turned on the television. She flicked through the guide for a minute or two before settling on a cooking show where contestants were grilling steaks and baking pecan pies in huge fire pits.

Tom watched it with her until he dozed off again.

His pre-paid phone began to buzz.

He opened his eyes. The house was dark. The television was off. He was alone in the room.

He dragged the phone out of his pocket after a bit of a struggle and looked at it. The time was a few minutes short of six A.M. He'd slept through the night in the recliner. The others must have decided to leave him there.

"Faust."

"Tom, it's Trish. We've got a situation report. Bad news. Mister Weir's talking to Bill right now. I said I'd call you."

"What's going on?" Tom asked, coming fully awake.

"We have reason to believe your location's been exposed. An inside source shared the address with a person we believe is Craig Norwood."

"Shit." Tom thought about Norwood already here, lurking around outside, sizing them up, planning his next move.

"I wonder if—"

A very loud explosion outside the house cut him off in mid-sentence.

CHAPTER 59

Staked out behind the tree across the street, Norwood crouched as shrapnel from the exploded car flew everywhere, making a sound like metallic rain after an insane thunderclap. Flames crackled and rippled.

According to the schedule in his head, that was likely the Suburban he'd just blown to kingdom come. They'd made the fundamental mistake of establishing a pattern, enabling Norwood to predict how he would need to protect himself from them.

As a result, he'd spent yesterday shopping for the ingredients to make IEDs, and he'd put them together last night. This morning, he'd planted two at each of the three intersections controlling access to the street.

One vehicle down; two to go.

His focus turned to the house. Using his monocular spy glass, he could see movement behind the living room curtains. He wanted to hit the place while they were still in it.

His equipment was spread out on the lawn beside him. He picked up the M72 rocket launcher and, balancing it on his thighs, removed the front and back caps and extended the tube.

He stood up and, pushing the safety forward to disengage it, balanced the launcher on his shoulder and squinted down the rear and front sights.

He pulled the trigger.

There was a bit of a recoil as the rocket flew out of the tube. There was also a fiery blast out the rear of the launcher, and Norwood heard glass breaking in the house behind him.

Because of the recoil, the muzzle of the launcher jumped upward slightly. He'd been aiming for the living room window, but as he watched in awe, the rocket took off the upper storey of the house. Boards and material flew high in the air, flames and smoke erupted, and floorboards collapsed down into the main level.

He hesitated for a moment, admiring his handiwork, then tossed the launcher aside and picked up his assault rifle. He already carried a handgun in a holster on his hip and, of course, his knife in its sheath. Before starting across the street, though, he stopped and looked both ways.

The other two surveillance cars were coming on hard, one from each direction. The Escape wheeled around the corner of Swanston and stopped behind the burning Suburban. Norwood triggered the second IED and the Escape leapt into the air in a burst of smoke and flame, rolling over several times onto the boulevard.

Norwood looked the other way. The Corolla had reached the intersection at Juliet Road. He set off both IEDs at once, delivering a one-two punch to the car that demolished it on the spot.

Having eliminated their external threats, he trotted across the street and up the stairs onto the verandah. The force of the rocket had blown off the screen door and front door. He kicked these aside and, high-stepping through the front entry, sprayed the living room with bullets.

No one there.

He heard the back screen door slamming shut, and feet thumping down the porch stairs. They were trying to escape through the backyard.

He fired a few shots down the hallway. Someone fired back at him.

Clambering over the broken doors, Norwood went back outside and down the driveway along the side of the house. There was a tall privacy fence closing off the back yard. The gate was fastened with a black wrought-iron latch.

Adrenaline pulsing, his targets mere meters away, Norwood used the assault rifle to blast the latch into oblivion. He kicked the gate open and strode inside, swinging the assault rifle around as he searched for the person with the hand gun.

There! The middle-aged, pudgy smoker. Norwood levelled his weapon.

He heard something beside him, and as he turned his head—

CHAPTER 60

When the rocket struck the house, Tom and Bill were in the hallway, shepherding their two protectees toward the rear exit. Lona Martin had already tumbled outside to clear the backyard for them.

The force of the blast blew Napier out through the screen door and over the porch railing onto the grass. He held his laptop up over his head to prevent it from being damaged.

Elaine followed, crashing into the verandah post and collapsing in a heap. Tom limped out and helped her down to ground level. Bill crouched as automatic gunfire raked the hallway, and he squeezed off a few rounds in reply.

"He's going back outside," Bill panted as he joined Tom at the bottom of the steps.

"He's coming around here," Tom said, waving at the gate. "You and Lona get them behind the garage."

Bill moved without hesitation.

Tom flattened himself against the privacy fence, listening to the sound of boots creaking down the driveway pavement. He leaned on his cane, fighting off a wave of dizziness.

The gate was hinged so that it would open inward.

He crouched, startled, as automatic gunfire blasted the latch into shards. A boot kicked the door open.

Norwood strode through, assault rifle levelled.

Tom swung his cane with all his might, striking Norwood on the bridge of his nose, knocking him down and out with a single blow.

Looking down at him, Tom kicked the rifle aside.

"I hope that hurts like hell, you son of a bitch."

Chapter 61

The fire department arrived almost immediately. Finding two houses burning across the street from each other, they called for reinforcements and got to work.

The Peterborough city police arrived only moments later and took over the job of clearing the victims from the scene. They set up a command centre on Swanston just off Armour Road, blocking off access to the neighbourhood from all directions. Two EMS ambulances arrived, parking nearby.

Tom stood next to Bill as they waited to be herded into police cruisers for the short ride up to the paramedics. He took the pistol from Bill's pocket and shoved it down the front of his pants.

"Better an ex-cop than a civilian housekeeper," he said when Bill gave him a stern look.

Napier was treated for scrapes and abrasions, and a few nasty wood splinters were pulled from his flesh and replaced with stitches. As the paramedic worked on him, Napier filmed the whole thing, narrating through clenched teeth like the pro that he was.

Elaine had a bump on her head from hitting the verandah

post. She was being examined for a concussion.

Lona was fine. She inquired around if anyone had some medicinal whisky. It was a nice try, Tom thought.

Bill also had a few splinters removed, and the paramedic treating him discovered that he'd somehow broken the little finger on his left (non-shooting) hand. As she reset the bone and put the finger into a splint, Bill grimaced at Tom.

"I've got no frigging idea how it happened."

"Tough guys never do," Tom replied.

He let a paramedic examine his foot and re-bandage it, since Lona was otherwise occupied. The gun that he'd shoved down the front of his pants was a Beretta Bobcat 21A mouse gun. It weighed only eleven and a half ounces, and was just under five inches in length. If the paramedic noticed it, he probably just thought Tom was having a good time.

His cane, by the way, was completely undamaged from its impact with Norwood's head. He decided it would be his constant companion from now on.

Which left Craig Norwood, who had a separate bus all to himself.

Tom moseyed over to watch. Norwood had regained consciousness, but was still groggy. His nose was being treated by a paramedic, who administered a local anaesthetic before shoving the bones and cartilage back into place. To his credit, Norwood didn't utter a sound. The paramedic inserted cotton into his nostrils and applied a bandage to hold the whole thing in place.

"Hurt much? Tom asked.

Norwood looked at him without expression.

"You didn't have to shoot me in the foot, you prick."

The corner of Norwood's mouth turned up slightly.

Tom was elbowed aside by Napier, all stitched up and festooned with band-aids. He held a paper and Sharpie in one hand, and his ubiquitous camera in the other.

"Craig! For chrissakes, it is you! What the hell, man?"

Norwood bared his teeth but held his silence.

"All you had to do was ask me, and we could have talked it over."

Norwood shook his head.

"Look, man. I don't take this personally. I mean, I know it was personal, but I'm not going to hold a grudge. Not if you agree to let me tell your story."

"Fuck off," Norwood murmured.

"No, no. Hear me out."

"Napier," Tom said. "Leave him alone."

"You're missing the point. We want him to talk. We *need* him to talk."

"If you keep badgering him, he's going to shut his mouth for good. Then nobody will get anything out of him."

"It'll all come out anyway," Napier said to Norwood. "You're looking at serious time already for what you've done today, what you did to Irwin and presumably to Judd, and when they reopen Sally's disappearance they'll use DNA evidence or whatever to connect you to that, too."

Norwood made a rude noise.

Tom turned around and saw Paisley and Leonard approaching. Their grace period was over now, apparently. Kate Greene was probably not far behind, and everything would have to be turned over to her.

"Okay," Napier said, "anyway, think about it. I can probably see to it that a percentage of the net earnings finds its way to your wife and kids. I'm not promising anything of course. This is not a verbal agreement. There are laws against that sort of thing. But think about it."

Tom turned away. There was, indeed, a law in Ontario that made sure any money earned by convicted criminals through a book or film contract would be turned over to the victims of their crimes. Napier's blatant offer to circumvent that law didn't sit well with Tom as a former police detective and major case manager.

Limping on his cane, he made his way slowly over to a city police SUV with its hatch open. He sat down on the ledge and leaned his head against the side beam. Closing his eyes, he hoped that Kate would get here soon.

He wanted to go home.

CHAPTER 62

Where do you confront a traitor? In a boardroom, at a long mahogany table set with bottles of water and orange juice, tablets and cellphones? Governed by Robert's Rules of Order, with a chair to direct the meeting, someone to take minutes, and a collection of folks empowered to vote yea or nay on the traitor's just deserts?

Or in a public place, such as a park bench downtown or maybe in an outdoor café on a quiet side street? Informal; open-ended; exposed to the harsh light of day or the wind and rain or whatever else is happening out in the real world?

It depends on what you want to do with him. And who gets to call the shots.

At the end of the day, Sean Cage called the shot. Despite his affability and sense of humour, Sean was not a nice man. He hadn't been raised to be a nice man. As a boy, he'd been tough and hard-nosed. He'd learned to survive on the streets of Bethnal Green by doing what needed to be done. As a young man, he'd used those street skills to navigate the markets and back alleys of Dacca on behalf of MI6, a city so densely populated it ranked seventh in the world in terms of souls per square kilometer, and much lower than that in terms of favourite travel destinations.

He'd brought that gristle and attitude to Canada with him, and he'd made a special point of shaping his company's culture around it. The Cage Intelligence Group hired only the toughest, the brightest, and the best. If a mistake was made, if someone was hired who turned out to be more concerned with themselves than the goals of the company—to the point of selling information to outside buyers, say—then CIG reacted the same way Sean Cage would.

Cage figured he owed Tom a favour for having gotten him shot in the foot, so he gave him the job of confronting the traitor in whatever manner he chose before the company handed down its penalty.

Tom chose the park bench route. Cage would have gone with a knife between the ribs in a dark alley, but a promise was a promise.

It was the last day of May. St. James Park was in full spring splendour. Bordered by Jarvis Street, Adelaide Street and King Street East, it offered a natural retreat from the Anglican expectations of St. James Cathedral a few meters to the west on King. One could wander in, sit down, stare at the well-kept gardens, and consider how God's eternal glory may be witnessed in a single flower.

Jeremy Dunaway was already waiting on the park bench when Tom arrived. His nose, predictably, was in his phone, his finger flicking as he scrolled through some feed or other. He looked up when Tom's shadow fell across his lap.

"There you are. I've been waiting." He tapped his phone into sleep mode and put it in his jacket pocket.

Tom sat down on the bench beside him, his cane held between his knees. He'd decided to call the cane Edgar, in honour of his late maternal grandfather Edgar Todd, who'd collected them. He'd died when Tom was eight, but he'd listened to enough stories about him to last a lifetime. Todd had been a game warden in Frontenac County, and in one story he'd owned a sword cane as part of his collection. While walking in the brush one day, he was said to have used it to fend off a mother bear he'd accidentally surprised with her cubs.

Edgar it was.

It wasn't a sword cane (he'd checked to make sure), but it was a hell of a baseball bat in a pinch.

"You put me in harm's way," Tom said.

Jeremy leaned back. "I don't know what you're talking about."

"Not only me, but King, Martin, Napier, and Elaine."

Jeremy snorted.

"And cost the lives of two other operatives, thanks to Norwood's IEDs."

"Why are we here, Faust? I've got work to do."

"We're here because Sean's given me the details of your next assignment, and I'm supposed to pass them on to you."

"Assignment? I already have a job."

"In two hours, you'll board a plane to Gaborone."

"What? Where?"

"Botswana. When you arrive you'll be met by Mister West, who'll take you to our office downtown. He'll leave you there with our station chief, whose name I wasn't told. The station chief will have arranged for a room for you somewhere nearby, and he'll explain your new duties."

"What the *hell* are you talking about, Faust?"

"I don't like being sold out, you smarmy little shit. I don't like bastards who talk out of both sides of their mouth and put my life on the line for a fucking money transfer."

They both looked up at the two men who had strolled over to their bench while Tom was talking. They were both approximately Jeremy's age, but not Jeremy's type. They were obvious gym rats. One, the guy with the shaved head, wore a navy windbreaker, unzipped, with a black polo shirt and jeans. The other, an Asian whose hair was dyed blond, edged his yellow cardigan sweater back to show the collapsible baton clipped to his belt.

"Go with these guys," Tom said. "They'll take you where you need to be."

The air seemed to leak out of Jeremy as he gave up the pretence of not knowing what was going on. "I was never good enough to satisfy them. There was always something wrong. What they pay me is an insult."

Tom used Edgar to leverage himself upright.

As Jeremy stood up, Tom punched him in the mouth with as much force as he could muster.

Jeremy went down like a sack of potatoes and stayed down.

Tom curled his lip. "If I ever see you again, you son of a bitch, I'll kill you.

The gym rats bent over to check on their prisoner as Tom strode purposefully away.

PART FOUR

ENDINGS

Tom and Kelly enjoyed a leisurely brunch the following Sunday morning. She'd been introduced to Swedish music while on tour, and a solo piano composition entitled "Valse élégiaque" played on the church's sound system as they dawdled over coffee. It was written by a woman named Laura Valborg Aulin, a music teacher from Örebro, born in 1860, who'd studied under Massenet and, as far as Tom was concerned, should have written a lot more music than she did. It was very pleasant stuff.

These days, his various wounds required much less attention. The knife cut on his neck was reduced to a red mark that was slowly fading away. His foot was also much better, although he still walked with a limp and always kept Edgar close at hand, particularly when navigating stairs. His scrapes on the head and chin from Cliff's shotgun, the hospital washroom floor, and the fender of the Bronco were gone.

Kelly had invoked her rights as a nurse practitioner to supervise the care of his foot and to insist that he submit, like a good dog, to physiotherapy that would strengthen the muscles and restore range of motion in his foot. Tom went along with it to keep her happy, but noticed an improvement soon after he began and obediently stuck with it.

"I have a little story to tell you," she said, pouring more coffee for them both. It was, of course, the Sumatra Mandhelling Tom had discovered through the late Judd Hendrick; he now had a cupboard filled with burlap sacks from the Gold Seal Coffee Company in Toronto. Surprisingly, Kelly had also developed a taste for it.

"A story? Fire away."

"While we were in Malmö," she began, "Aunt Nancy met a very nice lady named Monica Hellman. She's a professor of environmental studies at the University of Toronto."

"Uh oh," Tom said.

"No, actually they hit it off right away. They disagree on a whole bunch of stuff, naturally," she rolled her eyes, "but for some reason they took an instant liking to each other and Aunt Nancy was surprisingly cordial."

"That *is* a surprise." Tom sipped his coffee. Curmugeons usually weren't his thing, but Aunt Nancy occupied a special place in his heart, if for no other reason than the fact that she held him in high regard. Underneath the crust, she was a sweetheart.

"Anyway, Professor Hellman has been appointed head of the Environmental Science department at Trent, and she'll be moving to Peterborough this summer. She's a widow, so it's just her."

"How old is she?"

Kelly frowned. "I'm not sure. Late fifties, I'd say."

"Okay."

"Well, this is the part you won't believe. They've stayed in touch, and Aunt Nancy offered to share the house with her if she might be interested."

"Good lord!"

She laughed. "Yeah, I know. Crazy thing is, though, I think it might work out. Aunt Nancy still misses Aunt Alice, and she needs fresh intellectual stimulus, if you know what I mean, to keep her brain healthy and agile. Having someone around who disagrees with her a lot, in a very nice way, would be good for her."

"Yeah, I can see that." Tom was amused by the whole thing. Nancy and Alice had had some entertaining debates, particularly after Alice started dipping into the gin and singing arias from *La Traviata* in a loud voice. If this Hellman woman could fill that void, even partially, it would be a very good thing for the house on Homewood Avenue.

He realized Kelly had been watching him. When she raised her eyebrows, he smiled brainlessly.

"Oh, you're such a . . . such a *man*!" she declared in mock exasperation. "Thick as a brick."

"What am I thick about. . ." he trailed off as suspicion suddenly hit him. "What are you trying to say, Slender as a Reed?"

"I thought I'd give them a week." She watched him over the rim of her cup. "If they don't kill each other, you and I could take a shot at setting up shop together." She looked around. "I love this place."

It took him a moment. It had always been something that had been on the table, but there'd always been Aunt Nancy to think of. Now . . .

Grinning, he pulled out his phone.

"Tom, who are you calling?"

He winked at her. "U-Haul. Time to rent a moving van."

ENDING #2

Norwood was bored. Kenny Napier had been here for twenty minutes already and he was still dicking around, showing his permits and setting up cameras and testing the lighting and all that other crap. At this rate, it would take all afternoon. Norwood wanted to go back to his cell and stretch out for a little rest.

His lawyer was a very expensive dude who went by the name of McKenzie Danielson. "Call me Mack."

Norwood believed that Devoir, the darknet entity who'd handled most of his assignments, had arranged for Danielson to represent him in his current predicament. In their first meeting, the attorney had issued a strong warning not to talk about his international assignments. What he said about domestic hits was entirely up to him, but any mention of overseas work would bring the fury of Hell raining down on him.

Realizing that all Devoir's contracts were for international hits, Norwood had put two and two together. Danielson was Devoir's associate and shield. The other brokers who handled Canadian stuff could look out for themselves. Norwood was more than willing to go along with it; he hoped to be able to reconnect with Devoir once he was out and get back into business as soon as possible.

After that had been cleared away, Norwood wanted to talk about external arrangements, but Danielson had something else on his mind.

"We're a little upset, Craig. We need an explanation."

"Upset? Why?"

"We need you to clear up something for us. What you say will determine whether or not we have a future together."

"Sure. I understand. What is it?"

"What happened, Craig? What made you cross the line here? It seems like you went completely irrational. Is this something that'll happen again?"

Norwood paused before responding. He knew he'd have to answer for his actions sooner or later, and he'd spent a lot of time on his cot, staring at the ceiling, framing an explanation.

"It wasn't like me," he began. "Part of the problem was that it was personal, and I just lost it at some point. Quick answer: no more personal shit, so no more problems."

"I see." Danielson digested this for a moment before frowning. "A *rocket launcher*?"

"Yeah." Norwood laughed humourlessly. "Like I said, I just lost it."

"You lost control of yourself."

"Yeah," he murmured, knowing it was a bad thing to admit, but not seeing any way to sugar-coat it.

"And you say it won't happen again."

"Yeah."

"Let's move on. We're looking at a list of charges almost as long as my arm."

Norwood said nothing.

"I don't believe the murder charge for Dessler will stick. They can place your van at the Trent Hills farm, but they can't put you in it at the time of the murder, they can't put the crossbow in your hands or your finger on the trigger. Miraculously, no physical evidence and no witnesses. That part was actually well done, Craig. Despite being completely unhinged."

Norwood nodded.

"Stabbing Faust in the neck and shooting him in the foot are another matter, however. Faust will provide all the testimony the Crown will need to convict you on all the charges connected to those two incidents." He looked at Norwood. "This is where your, ah, loss of control really began to manifest itself."

"Yes."

"Then we have all the other Peterborough stuff. Break-and-enter in the apartment building, possession of prohibited weapons, discharging said weapons, five counts of attempted murder, charges relating to the IEDs and two homicides as a result, and other various miscellaneous things thrown in."

"I'm willing to deal."

"Fortunately for you, I'm a skilled and experienced negotiator." He smiled without humour. "Let's look at the list and come up with a strategy."

As it worked out, Norwood pleaded guilty to some of the charges, and in exchange the Crown agreed to drop the others.

Because he had no prior record of any kind, they were all first offences, and he had done his best to project an image of a simple carpenter who'd temporarily gone off the deep end, he ended up with a total sentence of twenty years, which he would serve in Millhaven Penitentiary. He'd be eligible for parole after twelve.

As soon as he was released, of course, he'd become Paul

Nelson and, after disappearing, make a beeline for Yucatán.

This morning, he met with Danielson again to finalize other arrangements. He'd made it clear earlier on, when agreeing to the plea deal, that he wanted his family taken care of and was willing to pay the attorney well for his services in this regard. Danielson agreed, after hearing some numbers.

Sharon visited him not long after his incarceration. She was upset, of course, but the experience of having been brought down from Renfrew in a limo with a uniformed driver and a high-powered attorney had helped to improve her mood a bit. It took a while for Norwood to convince her that it would be necessary for her and the girls to leave the country, but again, she eventually came on board once he'd explained to her the place he was setting up for them.

This morning, he and Danielson had finalized those plans and shaken hands on the deal. Norwood provided him with the specifics of a bank account in the Caymans, number and passwords, and Danielson would proceed with the purchase of a lovely little property in Cuzamá, Yucatán, just southeast of the capital city of Mérida.

The account contained just over $5 million USD, which would be transferred to a local account Danielson would open for Norwood in the name of Paul Nelson, the external alias he would use going forward. Danielson would take a million bucks from the account as his fee for services rendered.

Norwood had other offshore accounts, of course, but Danielson didn't need to know that.

The place he was buying for Sharon and the girls cost just under a million US. It was a restored hacienda on fifteen acres. It had four bedrooms, three bathrooms, air conditioning, a big fireplace and propane heating, a solar panel system that heated water for the showers, a sewage treatment system that was part of an expensive ecosystem project, and an outdoor pool. It had two corrals for horses and a stable, a chicken coop, and its own winery.

More than enough to keep Sharon busy.

Plus it had a private cenote on the property.

What the hell was a cenote? he asked himself.

Turns out it was a deep water well, half-hidden in a cavern or a system of caverns. The water was used for livestock and swimming and all sorts of other great things. The cavern was one of those deals with stalactites and stalagmites and fish and frogs and that sort of stuff. The agent said he thought there was a bunch of caverns down there. Apparently the Cuzamá area was famous for these cenotes, and they were a big tourist attraction. This one he would have all to himself.

He couldn't wait to get down there.

Meanwhile, he had to play nice with little Kenny this afternoon.

Their first meeting had included Danielson, as they talked about the scope of Kenny's proposed film, what would be expected of Norwood in terms of availability and level of co-operation: that sort of thing.

Napier had initially wanted to include footage of Norwood in jail as part of the thing he was shooting as an add-on to his book, but he'd changed his mind and decided on a separate piece focused exclusively on Norwood. That involved a lot of discussion with Danielson, who explained that Norwood would not confess to any crimes other than the ones to which he'd already pleaded guilty.

Napier wasn't happy, because he'd shot a lot of footage of the conflagration at Snelgrove Road and wanted to put it to good use. After much whining and bitching and carping, however, he wrote it up the way they wanted it.

Norwood's only decision now was to figure out how much bullshit he'd spin and how much he'd give Napier that was close enough to the truth to sound good.

One thing he wouldn't talk about was Sally. Napier clearly wanted to probe that one, given his schoolboy crush on her back then, but Norwood wasn't going to give him the time of day on that subject.

It was too disturbing, even now. She'd found out he was trying his hand at selling weed around the school and threatened to spill the beans. Trying to force him to stop. They argued, she threatened to tell Mr. Collins, the neighbour who'd been kind to him. He was the only person in town who thought well of him, and the threat upset him. She got mouthy about it, he saw red and hit her, and when his vision cleared he'd hit her too many times and she was dead.

His father was at work; his mother was sleeping after a long night shift; he loaded the body into his mother's car and had to go back inside for the keys. Which is when the little snotnose Kenny had rode up on his bike. He probably knew all along what had happened, but was too scared of Norwood to say anything. Little arse.

He might be able to find out now. Napier might say something to give himself away.

"Are you ready, Craig?" Napier asked, standing behind one of his tripods.

"You bet I am."

ENDING **#3**

Jeremy Dunaway had been in Gaborone for two weeks before the boom was lowered.

It came during a lunch meeting with Nicholas West, Cage's vice president of Intelligence and the man who'd escorted him here to CIG's Botswana field office. They went to the Wimpy restaurant just up the street from the Canadian consulate. Neither of them was particularly interested in facing Botswana cuisine that day, so while West ordered a Big Champion burger with Coke, Jeremy had hake fillets and chips. It was all pretty lousy fare, but Jeremy was too upset to notice.

As they ate, West chatted about the various tourist spots of interest in the country, maintaining a pleasant atmosphere throughout the meal. Jeremy was mostly silent, knowing that the hammer was about to drop on his head.

Finally, when the last bites were eaten, West patted his lips and leaned back. "Security will escort you back into the building so you can gather up your things. We'll need your key lock cards, company ID, and all that."

"You're firing me?"

"The lease for your apartment has been cancelled, so you'll

have to get out tomorrow."

"I don't believe this."

"Actions have consequences, Mister Dunaway."

"But I'm nearly broke!"

"Your severance has already been deposited in your account."

His wonderful and extremely generous severance pay turned out to be ten thousand Botswana pula, which converted to a few bucks over one thousand Canadian dollars.

He had very few personal belongings, so it took little time to pack his knapsack and clear out. He had nowhere to go. He had about fifty dollars' worth of pula in his wallet, so he bought a newspaper and found a restaurant where he could drink bottled Coke and look for another place to live. And a job.

It was a problem that he was white and that he didn't speak Tswana, although English was fairly common in the capital. He saw opportunities for casual labourers, but they were advertised as being open only to Botswana citizens. There was also an ad for a company looking for five IT officers that was only commission-based and probably involved some kind of telephone sales or that kind of crap, but he circled it anyway for follow-up.

In the apartments for rent column, he saw an ad for a one-bedroom flat in a neighbourhood that he'd learned was not very good. The rent was cheap, though. The kicker? Along with the address, the ad said: "Ask for Neo."

Neo. The One. A picture of Keanu Reaves as his landlord filled his mind.

He used his phone to call up a city map and set the GPS to guide him there after a quick stop at his bank to withdraw more money. He intended to pay Neo for his rent in advance.

He was four blocks from his destination when a gang of kids

mugged him. They were somewhat less than gentle.

When he managed to regain his feet, he was dizzy and his knee hurt where someone had stomped on it. He had cuts around his mouth and on his forehead, and his clothing was torn and filthy from rolling around on the ground trying to protect himself from their shockingly hard feet.

His wallet and his phone were gone. His pockets were turned out. Empty.

For chrissakes, his shoes were gone. Clark's desert boots, nearly new. They'd cost him over $200.

He had little choice but to keep on going to his destination, hoping that Neo would take pity on him and bail him out.

Neo was a woman.

Come to find out that Neo was a common female name that translated as "gift." She was middle-aged and overweight, but sharp as a knife. She was also eccentric enough to believe that installing a young white man, and a fairly attractive one at that, under her roof might bring good luck to her various enterprises.

Jeremy ended up in a small, one-room flat on the top floor of Neo Moseki's building. Thanks to the swarm of kids who'd mugged him and stolen his wallet, he didn't have enough left in his bank account to buy a plane ticket out of there, so he settled in and tried to make the best of it.

Neo found him a job doing dishes in a nearby restaurant, a cluttered flytrap called The Lion Den that served local cuisine to the working poor. He was able to make enough to pay his rent and put food in his belly.

Eventually he grew used to eating stuff like *bogobe jwa lerotse*, a porridge made with lerotse melon; *samp*, a coarse corn hominy served as samp and beans; and mopane worms in peanut sauce. The sauce was thankfully hot and spicy. Without it, the worms tended to taste like cooked cardboard.

There was also plenty of beer. There were two kinds, clear and opaque. Clear beer was more expensive and often consumed by tourists; on pay day Jeremy treated himself to a case of Castle and a bag of magwinya, sweet dough balls. Later in the week it was Chibuku, the most popular opaque beer brewed from corn and sorghum. Either one, if consumed in quantity, would give him a satisfactory buzz.

For a while, he considered suicide. His former life in Canada was a fading memory, and he'd given up hope of ever going home again. He could just walk out into the Kalahari and keep on going. Let the planet reclaim his molecules.

The next stage was apathy. Who gave a fuck? The food was crap, but it was cheap and plentiful. No one cared if he hauled case after case of Castle or Lion up to his room and got drunk in front of the television set every night. What the hell, right?

One afternoon while he was washing dishes the owner, a man named Gaione Tau, came back with a little guy in a worn-out brown suit.

"He wants to talk to you."

Jeremy squinted through the steam.

"Only a few minutes," the little guy said.

Jeremy looked at Gaione. "All right with you?"

"Yeah sure. Few minutes."

Wiping his hands on his apron, Jeremy followed them out to a table at the back of the restaurant. Gaione brought them two bottles of Lion opaque beer.

"I am paying," said the little guy.

"What did you want to see me for?"

"You were hard to find. I expected you to be working

somewhere in the diamond industry."

"A question of contacts. I don't have any." Other than sweet Neo, he silently added.

"I see. Well, let me start by saying I'm aware of what has been done to you."

"You are, huh?" Jeremy took a big swig. The aftertaste was horrible, but it quenched the thirst. "Just who are you, anyway?"

"My name is Parth Anand. I work for the Botswana office of a company based in New Delhi. We do IT work, the sort of thing you did in Canada."

"What do you know about what I did in Canada, Mister Anand?"

"Just about everything, I suppose."

Jeremy drained his bottle, staring at him. "Does the name Tom Faust mean anything to you?"

"Yes, as a matter of fact it does."

Jeremy looked up as Gaione set another bottle of beer next to his elbow and winked at him before slouching back into the kitchen.

"What exactly are you trying to say to me?"

"We have a job for you," Parth said. "If you're interested. It would mean returning to Canada, though. I'm not sure you would want this."

"Oh, I want it all right." Swig. "So, you're Indian Intelligence, right? Which agency, exactly? RAW?"

The Research and Analysis Wing was India's foreign intelligence agency. They spied on the military, political, and scientific operations of other countries with a view to protecting India's vested interests in these areas.

Parth smiled politely. "Oh, you are very clever. But these

are questions that will only be answered in New Delhi."

Jeremy sighed. "I'm flat busted, Mister Anand. I can't afford a plane ticket to the other side of the room, never mind India."

Parth patted his rumpled suit coat pocket. "It's already here. And accommodations somewhat better than your present arrangement with Mrs. Moseki, may the heavens bless her."

"When do we leave?"

"As soon as you shake Mister Tau's hand and hang up that charmingly tatty apron of yours."

"Wait. One last question. Why did you bring up Faust?"

Parth made a face. "This was perhaps a mistake, but since you seem to have accepted our job offer—you have accepted it, correct?"

"Fucking right I have."

"Yes, well, in light of your acceptance I may not be punished if I let slip that your assignment will centre on Mister Faust, the former police detective."

"Faust? Why him?"

"We have reason to believe he'll be assigned to something that may interfere with a project of ours in your wonderful country. We'll need you to do something about that."

"You mean, you want me to take Tom Faust out of the picture?"

"Yes."

"Permanently?"

"If that becomes necessary. Yes."

Jeremy reached across the table and shook Anand's hand.

Oxford Station, ON
January 29, 2025

ACKNOWLEDGMENTS

On April 13, 2024, I gave a talk at the library in Mallorytown, Ontario, held by the Friends of the Front of Yonge Public Library. The volunteers were terrific, and the audience was receptive and engaged. At one point I asked for their opinion on stories that are told from the point of view of the bad guy. They were unanimous that they liked reading this kind of thing, so I promised to give it a shot. Here you go, folks.

Information about Toronto's PATH system may be found in Debra Mackinnon, Stefam Treffers, and Randy K. Lippert, "Moving Through Toronto's PATH: Assembling private urban governance," *Urban Studies*, vol. 61, Issue 14, 2795 - 2816.

Information about Botswana cuisine may be found in the article by Omo Ohiokpehai entitled, "Nutritional Aspects of Street Foods in Botswana," *Pakistan Journal of Nutrition*, 2 (2): 76-81 (2003).

I should mention that at one time I lived at 748 Snelgrove Road in Peterborough. We moved there the summer before I began attending Trent University. I have absolutely nothing against the place. I certainly never wanted to blow it up with a rocket launcher, but there you go.

Special thanks once again to Reg and Kathy Coffey, Tom Van Dusen, and many others who continue to read my books and support my work. I'm greatly appreciative.

As always, I wouldn't be where I am today without the love and guidance of my lifetime partner, Lynn L. Clark. Chin up, love. I know it's not fair that Norwood may get to go to Mexico while we can't afford to, but you never know. This one may end up being the ship we've been waiting for, sailing into our harbour with cash for a lifetime.

ABOUT THE AUTHOR

Michael J. McCann lives and writes in Oxford Station, Ontario, Canada. A graduate of Trent University (Peterborough, ON) and Queen's University (Kingston, ON), he served as Production Editor of *Criminal Reports (Third Series)* and Law Reports Co-ordinator for Carswell Legal Publications (Western) before spending fifteen years at the Canada Border Services Agency as a project officer and national program manager. He's married to author Lynn L. Clark. They have one son.

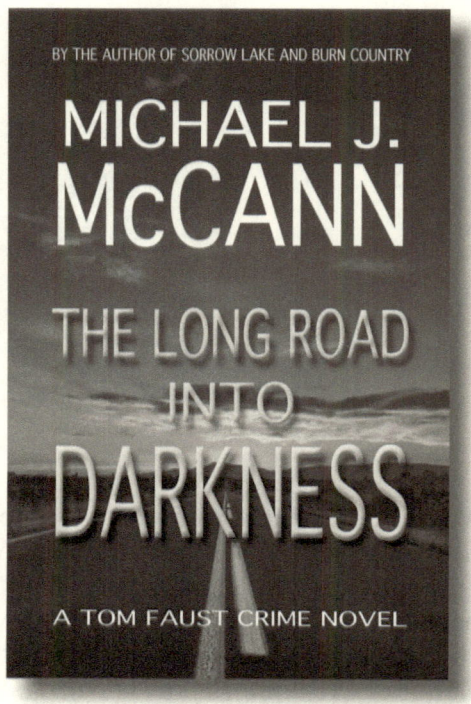